Benjamin smiled and closed the gap that had formed between them and placed a hand on Freya's slender hip.

"We don't have to like each other to be good together...and I think we could be *very* good together. Marry me and you'll have everything you would have had if you had married Javier."

"And you get continued revenge," she finished for him, her tone contemptuous.

"*Exactement.* We *both* get what we want."

She could smell the warmth of his skin beneath the freshness of his cologne...

Benjamin was *not* what she wanted. She wouldn't be swapping one rich man for another, she would be swapping ice for fire, safety for danger, all the things she had never wanted.

She clamped her lips together to contain a gasp.

Benjamin had taken another step closer. Their bodies were almost flush.

She closed her eyes and breathed in deeply, trying to block her dancing senses and contain what was happening within her frame.

"You know what this means?" he murmured.

She swallowed and managed a shake of her head.

"It means you and I are now betrothed. Which means we need to seal the deal."

Before she could guess what he meant, he'd hooked an arm around her waist and pulled her tight against him. Before she could protest, he'd covered her mouth with his.

Rings of Vengeance

Three vengeful billionaires, three scandalous weddings!

Benjamin Guillem was once Luis and Javier Casillas's closest friend. Until the day the brothers stole from him. Now they are enemies, and nothing and no one will stand in the way of their revenge!

And if that means stealing, bartering or buying a bride, then so be it!

But with the marriage vows spoken, can these new brides unravel their billionaires' games of vengeance, and bring these three powerful tycoons to their knees?

Find out more in:

Benjamin and Freya's story

Billionaire's Bride for Revenge

And look out for Luis's and Javier's stories

Coming soon!

Michelle Smart

—

BILLIONAIRE'S BRIDE FOR REVENGE

HARLEQUIN PRESENTS®

Recycling programs
for this product may
not exist in your area.

ISBN-13: 978-1-335-50440-1

Billionaire's Bride for Revenge

First North American publication 2018

Copyright © 2018 by Michelle Smart

Printed in U.S.A.

Michelle Smart's love affair with books started when she was a baby, when she would cuddle them in her cot. A voracious reader of all genres, she found her love of romance established when she stumbled across her first Harlequin book at the age of twelve. She's been reading—and writing—them ever since. Michelle lives in Northamptonshire, England, with her husband and two young Smarties.

Visit the Author Profile page at Harlequin.com for more titles.

This is for Tilly & Eliza. Follow your dreams xxx

CHAPTER ONE

BENJAMIN GUILLEM CAST his eye over the heads of the people scattered around the landscaped garden of the Tuscan-style villa in the heart of Madrid, an easy feat considering he was a head taller than most. The only guest there without a plus-one, he was also the only guest in attendance with no intention of celebrating Javier Casillas's engagement.

He snatched a flute of champagne from a passing waitress and drank it in one swallow. The bubbles felt like jagged barbs down his throat, magnifying the hot, knotted feeling that twisted inside him.

Javier and Luis had betrayed him. The Casillas brothers had taken advantage of their lifelong friendship and ripped him off. All the documentary evidence pointed to that inescapable conclusion.

He hoped the evidence was wrong. He hoped his instincts were wrong. They had to be. The alternative was too sickening to contemplate.

He would not leave this party until he knew the truth.

Benjamin took another champagne and stepped over to the elaborate fountain for a better view. He spotted Luis at the far end of the garden surrounded by his usual entourage of sycophants. Javier, Luis's non-identical twin brother and host of the party, was proving far more elusive.

Javier would be hating every minute of this party. He was the most antisocial person Benjamin knew. He'd always been that way, even before their father killed their mother over two decades ago.

Thoughts of the Casillas brothers swiftly evaporated when a dark-haired woman walked out of the summer room, capturing his attention with one graceful step onto the flourishing green lawn. She raised her face to the sky and closed her eyes, holding the pose as if trying to catch the sun's rays on her skin. There was an elegance about her, a poise, a way of holding herself that immediately made him think she was a dancer.

There were a lot of dancers there. Javier's new fiancée was the Principal Dancer at the ballet company the brothers had bought in their mother's memory. Benjamin wondered if the fiancée knew or cared that she was only a trophy to him.

Benjamin had never cared for the ballet or the people who inhabited its world. This dancer though…

The sun caught the red undertones of her hair, which hung in a thick, wavy mass over glimmering pale shoulders. Her features were interesting rather than classically pretty, a strong, determined jaw softened by a wide, generous mouth…

Her eyes suddenly found his, as if she sensed his gaze upon her, two black orbs ringing at him.

A slight frown appeared on her brow as she stared, an unanswerable question in it, a frown that then lessened as her generous mouth curved hesitantly.

His knotted stomach made a most peculiar twisting motion.

No, not classically pretty but striking. Mesmerising.

He couldn't look away.

And she couldn't seem to tear her gaze from him either, a moment in time existing only for them, two eye-locked strangers.

And then a shadow appeared behind her and she blinked, the sun-bound spell woven around them dissolving as quickly as it had formed.

The shadow was Javier emerging from the sunroom to join his own party.

He spotted Benjamin and nodded a greeting while his right hand settled proprietorially on the dancer's waist.

It came to him in an instant that this woman, the slowly forming smile on her face now frozen, was Javier's fiancée.

By the time Javier had steered the dancer to stand before him by the fountain, Benjamin had swallowed the bite of disappointment, shaken off the last of that strange spell and straightened his spine.

He wasn't here to party or for romance. He was here for business.

'Benjamin, it's good to see you,' Javier said. 'I don't think you've met my fiancée, Freya, have you?'

'No.' He looked straight at her. A hint of colour slashed her high cheekbones. 'A pleasure to meet you.'

Under different circumstances it *would* have been a pleasure but now the spell had broken all that remained was a faint distaste that she should have stared so beguilingly at him when engaged to another man.

But that was all the introduction Javier deemed necessary between his oldest friend and new fiancée, saying, 'Have you seen Luis yet?'

'Not yet but I am hoping to rectify that now.' Then, dismissing the striking vision from his consideration, Benjamin added evenly, 'We need to talk. You, me and Luis. In private.'

There was a momentary silence as Javier stared at him, eyes narrowing before he nodded slowly and caught the attention of a passing waiter. 'Find my brother and tell him to meet me and Senor Guillem in my study.' Dropping his hold on his fiancée's waist, he turned and strode back into the summer room without another word.

Two months later...

Smile, Freya, it's a party and all for a worthy cause.

Smile for the cameras. Smile for your fiancé, still not here but expecting you to turn on the charm even in his absence.

Smile for the gathered strangers, pretend you know them intimately, let them brush their cheek against yours as you greet each other with the fake air kisses that make your stomach curdle.

Smile, there's another camera. Smile as you nurse your glass of champagne.

Smile at the waiting staff circling the great ball-room with silver trays of delicious-smelling canapés but do not—not—be so gauche as to eat one.

Just. Smile.

And she did. Freya smiled so much her face ached, and then she smiled some more.

Being promoted to Principal Dancer at Compania de Ballet de Casillas came with responsibilities that involved more than pure dance. Freya was now the official face of the ballet company and at this, its most exciting time. The new state-of-the-art theatre the Casillas brothers were building for the company opened in a couple of months and it was her face on all the billboards and advertisements for it. She was the lead in the opening production.

Her, Freya Clements, an East London girl from a family so poor that winters were often a choice between heating and food, a Principal Dancer. It was a dream. She was living her dream. Marriage to Javier Casillas, joint owner of the ballet company, would be the...she almost thought icing on the cake but realised it was the wrong metaphor. Or was it the wrong simile? She couldn't remember, had always struggled to differentiate between them. Either way, she couldn't think of an appropriate metaphor or simile to describe her feelings about marrying Javier.

Javier was rich. Very, very rich. No one knew how much he and his twin Luis were worth but it was rare for their names to be mentioned in the press without the prefix *billionaire*. He was also handsome. He had chosen her to be, as he had put it, his life partner. When she looked at him she imagined him as her Prince Charming but without the title. Or the charm.

It didn't matter that he was morose and generally unavailable. It was better that way. Marrying him gave her deteriorating mother a fighting chance.

In exactly one week he would be her husband.

The entire ballet company was, as of that day, on a two-week shutdown so the new state-of-the-art training facilities and ballet school that went hand in hand with the new theatre could be completed. Javier had decreed they would fit their nuptials in then so as not to disturb her training routine.

Where was he? He should have been here an

hour ago. She'd snuck away to the Ladies to call him but found her phone not working. She couldn't think what was wrong with it but she had no signal and no Internet connection. She would try again as soon as she had a minute to herself.

The media were out in force tonight, ready for their first public glimpse of the couple, beside themselves that Javier, son of the ballet dancers Clara Casillas and Yuri Abramova, a union that had ended in tragedy and infamy, was to marry 'a ballerina with the potential for a career as stratospheric as his mother's had been'. That had been an actual quote in a highbrow Spanish magazine, translated by her best friend, fellow ballerina and flatmate, Sophie, who had mastered the Spanish language with an ease that made Freya ashamed of her own inadequacies. In the two years she had lived and worked in Madrid she had hardly picked up the basics of the language.

Many of the company's *corps de ballet* were in attendance that night, window dressing for the attending patrons of the arts whose money and patronage were wanted. Sophie had begged off with a migraine, something she'd been suffering with more frequently in recent weeks. Freya wished she were there. Just having Sophie in the same room soothed the nauseous panic nibbling in her stomach.

Just smile.

So she stretched her lips as wide and as high as she could and accepted yet another fake air kiss from another of Europe's richest women and tried not to choke on the cloud of perfume she inhaled with it.

A tall figure stepped into the ballroom of the hotel the fundraiser was being held in.

Her stomach swooped.

It was *him*. The man from her engagement party. *Benjamin Guillem.*

The name floated in her head before she could stamp it out.

It was a name that she had thought of far too often since the party two months ago. His face had found itself floating into her daydreams too many times for comfort too. And in her night dreams…

Suddenly aware of the danger she was placing herself in, she shifted her stance so he was no longer in her eyeline and smiled at an approaching elderly man.

She must *not* stare at him again. If he came over to speak to her she would smile gracefully exactly as she had to the other guests and this time she would find her tongue to speak in the clear voice she had cultivated through the years; chiselling the East London accent out of herself so no one in this moneyed world ever doubted she belonged.

She'd never been so tongue-tied before as she had the first time she'd seen him. She had literally been unable to say a word, just stared at him like some kind of goofball.

Her senses were on red alert, though, and as hard as she tried to concentrate on what the elderly man was saying—something about his granddaughter being a keen dancer—her skin prickled with electricity.

And then he was there, a step behind the old man, waiting his turn to speak to her.

She didn't look directly at him as she laughed politely at a joke the old man said. She hoped it was a joke. She could barely hear her own words let alone his. Blood pounded hot and hard in her head, a burning where Benjamin's gaze rested on her.

He was well mannered enough to wait for a natural pause in the conversation before stepping forward. 'Mademoiselle Clements?'

To her horror she found her vocal cords frozen again and could only nod her acknowledgement at the simple question.

'We met at your engagement party. I am Benjamin Guillem, an old friend of your fiancé.'

He had the thickest, richest French accent she had ever heard. It felt like set honey to her senses.

Unlike the other guests she'd met that evening he made no effort to pull her into an embrace, just stared at her with the eyes she'd found so unnervingly beautiful at her engagement party. Olive skinned, he had messy thick black hair and thick black eyebrows, a rough scar above the top lip of his firm mouth and a sloping nose. He reminded her of a *film noir* star, his dark handsome features carrying a disturbingly dangerous air. Where the other guests wore traditional tuxedos, Benjamin wore a black suit and black shirt with a skinny silver tie. If he were to produce a black fedora it wouldn't look out of place.

The only spot of colour on him were his eyes. Those devastating eyes. A clear, vivid green, they pierced through the skin. They were eyes that didn't miss a thing.

'I remember,' she said in as light a tone as she could muster, fighting through the thumping beats of her heart. 'You stole him away from me.' She'd been thankful for it. Javier had put his hand to her waist. His touch, a touch any other woman would no doubt delight in, had left her cold.

She prayed fervently that by the time they exchanged their vows in exactly seven days her feelings for her fiancé would have thawed enough for her to be receptive to his touch. Javier had yet to make a physical move on her but she knew that would change soon.

They both knew what they were getting into, she reminded herself for the hundredth time. Theirs would be a loveless marriage, the only kind of marriage either of them could accept. She would continue to dance and enjoy her flourishing career for as long as she wanted and then, when *she* felt the time was right, give him babies.

She would be Javier's trophy, she accepted that too, but was hopeful that once they got to know each other properly, friendship would blossom.

And even if friendship didn't blossom, marriage to Javier would be worth it. Anything had to be better than the pain of watching helplessly while her mother withered away. Marrying Javier gave her the chance to extend her mother's life and ensure it was a life worth living.

Benjamin inclined his head, those eyes never losing their hold on hers. 'Unfortunate but necessary. We had business that could not wait.'

'Javier said the same.' That was all he'd said when she had tentatively probed him on it when he'd returned to her an hour later. The tone in his voice had implicitly told her to ask no more.

Her fiancé was a book that wasn't merely closed but thickly bound too, impossible to open never mind read.

His disappearance with his brother and friend had only piqued her interest because of the friend. This friend. Benjamin. She'd had to hold herself back from peppering Javier with questions about him, something she'd found disturbing in itself.

It occurred to her that she was lucky she felt nothing for Javier. If her heart beat as rapidly for him as it did for this Frenchman she would have thought twice about accepting his proposal. She knew Javier would have thought twice about proposing if she'd displayed any sort of feelings for him too.

The Frenchman showed no sign of filling her in on their meeting either, raising a shoulder in what she assumed to be an apology.

'I'm sorry if you're looking for Javier but I'm afraid he hasn't arrived yet,' she said when the silence that fell between them stretched like charged elastic. She had to remind herself that people were watching her. 'I don't think Luis is here yet either.'

Benjamin studied her closely, looking for signs that Freya knew about the enmity between him and the Casillas brothers but there were no vibes of suspicion. He hadn't expected Javier to take her into his confidence. Javier did not do confidences.

But there *were* vibes emanating from her, as if her skin were alive with an electricity that sparked onto him, an intensity in her dark eyes he had to stop himself from being pulled into.

He had a job to do and could not afford the distraction of her striking sultriness to delay him at a moment when time was of the essence. He'd planned everything down to the minute.

Tonight, her dark hair had been pulled back into a tight bun circled with tiny round diamonds, her lithe figure draped in a sleeveless deep red crushed velvet dress that flared at the hip to fall mid-calf. Her pale bare shoulders glimmered under the ballroom lights just as they had done under the hot Madrid sun and there was an itch in the pads of his fingers to touch that silky looking skin.

He leaned in a little closer so only she could hear the words that would next spill from his tongue. The motion sent a little whirl of a sultry yet delicate fragrance darting into his senses. He resisted the urge to breathe it in greedily.

'I already know Javier isn't here. Forgive me, Mademoiselle Clements, but I have news that is only for your ears.'

A groove appeared in her forehead, the black eyes widening.

He turned his head pointedly to the huge swing doors that led out of the ballroom and held his elbow out. 'May I?'

Her throat moved before she nodded, then slipped her hand through the crook of his arm.

Benjamin guided her through the guests socialising magnificently as they waited for their hosts, the Casillas brothers, to arrive and for the fundraising gala to begin in earnest. They would have a long wait. The wheels he'd set in motion should, if all went as planned, delay them both for another hour each. He felt numerous eyes fall upon them and bit back a smile.

When Javier did finally get there, he would learn his fiancée had disappeared with his newly sworn enemy.

He had never wanted it to come to this but Javier and Luis had forced his hand. He'd warned them. After their last acrimonious meeting, he had given them a deadline and warned them failure to pay what was owed would lead to consequences.

Freya was collateral damage in the ugly mess *they* had created, the deceitful, treacherous bastards.

When they were in the hotel's lobby, Benjamin stopped beside a marble pillar to say, 'I am sorry for the subterfuge but Javier has encountered a problem. He does not wish to alarm the other guests but has asked me to bring you to him.'

'Is he hurt?' She had a husky voice that perfectly matched the sultriness of her appearance.

'No, it is not that. He is well. I only know that he has asked me to take you to him.'

He saw the hesitation in her eyes but gave her no chance to act on it, taking the hand still held in the crook of his arm and lacing his fingers through hers.

'Come,' he said, then began moving again, this time towards the exit doors.

Her much shorter, graceful legs kept pace easily.

A sharp pang of guilt punched his gut at her misplaced trust, a pang he dismissed.

This was Javier's fiancée.

Benjamin's sister, Chloe, worked as a seamstress at the ballet company and knew Freya. She had described her as nice if a little aloof. Intelligent. Too intelligent not to know exactly the kind of man she had chosen to marry.

Money and power in the world you inhabited were mighty aphrodisiacs, he thought scathingly.

What he found harder to dismiss were the evocative tingles seeping into his bloodstream from the feel of her hand in his and the movement of her lithe body sweeping along beside him.

His driver was waiting for them as arranged at the front of the hotel.

Benjamin waited until she was sitting in the car before following her in, staring straight into the security camera above the hotel's door as he did so.

'Do you really not know what kind of trouble Javier is in?' she asked with steady composure as the driver pulled away from the hotel.

'Mademoiselle Clements, I am merely your courier for this trip. All will be revealed when we reach our destination.'

'Where is he?'

'In Florence.'

'Still?'

'I understand there was some delay.' An understanding brought about by his own sabotage. Benjamin had paid an aviation official to conduct a spot-check of Javier's private plane with the promise of an extra ten thousand euros if he could delay him by two hours. He'd also paid a contact who worked for a mobile phone network to jam Freya's phone.

As they drove into the remote airfield less than ten minutes later she suddenly straightened. 'I haven't got my passport on me.'

'You don't need it.'

Benjamin's own private plane was ready to board, his crew in place, all ready to get the craft into the air the moment he and Freya were strapped in.

He ignored another wave of guilt as she climbed the metal steps onto his jet, as trusting as a spring lamb.

Within half an hour of leaving the hotel they were airborne.

He inhaled properly for what felt the first time in half an hour.

His plan had worked effortlessly.

Sitting on the reclining leather seat facing her, Benjamin watched Freya. Her features were calm, the only indication anything was worrying her the slight tapping of her fingers on her lap. He would put her out of her misery soon enough.

'Drink?' he asked.

Her eyes found his and held them for the longest time before blinking. 'Do you have tea?'

'I think something stronger.'

'Do I *need* something stronger?'

Not yet she didn't.

'No, but a drink will help you relax, *ma douce*.'

Her throat moved, the generous lips pulling together. Then she loosened her tight shoulders and nodded.

Benjamin summoned a member of his cabin crew. 'Get Mademoiselle Clements a drink, whatever she wants. I will have a glass of port.'

Soon their drinks had been served and Freya sipped at her gin and tonic. Her forehead was pressed to the window, her gaze fixed on the dark night sky. She covered her mouth and stifled a yawn.

'You are tired?' he asked politely.

A quick, soft shake of her head that turned into a nod that morphed into another yawn. When she met his gaze there was sheepish amusement in her eyes. 'Flying makes me sleepy. I'm the same in cars. Are you *sure* Javier is okay?'

'Very sure. Your seat reclines into a bed. Sleep if you need to.'

'I'll be fine, thank you.' Another yawn. Another sip of her drink.

He observed her fight to keep her eyes open, the lids becoming heavier followed by a round of rapid blinking, then heavying again.

A few minutes later her eyes stayed closed, her chest rising and falling in a gentle rhythm.

He leaned forward and carefully removed the glass from her slackening fingers.

Her eyes opened and stared straight into his.

A shot of something plunged into his heart and twisted.

Her lips curved in the tiniest of smiles before her eyes fluttered back shut.

Benjamin closed his eyes and took a long breath.

There was something about this woman he reacted to in a way he could not comprehend. It unnerved him.

Through all the legal battles he'd been going through these past two months and as the full extent of the Casillas brothers' treachery had become sickeningly clearer, Freya's face had kept hovering into his thoughts.

He stared at it now, watching her sleep through the dimmed cabin lights, absorbing the features that had played in his mind like a picture implanted into his brain.

It was fortuitous that she should sleep. It would make the difficult conversation they must have easier if they weren't thirty-five thousand feet in the air.

Let her have a little longer of oblivion before she learned she had been effectively kidnapped.

CHAPTER TWO

A BUSTLE OF movement in the cabin woke Freya from her light slumber to find Benjamin's gaze still on her.

A warm flush crept through her veins.

For the first time since infancy, full sleep hadn't taken her into its clutches.

He gave a tight smile. 'I was about to wake you. We will be landing shortly.'

'Sorry.' She smothered a yawn and stretched her legs, flexing her feet before noticing her shoes had slipped off. 'Travel has always had a sedative effect on me.'

It had been the case since she'd been a baby and her parents had taken turns walking her in the pram to get her to sleep. Once she had outgrown the pram the walks had continued with Freya in a buggy, sleeping happily along the same daily walk, which had taken them past a local ballet school. She had always woken up then. Her first concrete memory was pointing at the little girls in their pink tutus and squealing, 'Freya dance too!'

Those early walks had given birth to two things:

her love of dance and her unfailing ability to fall asleep in any mode of transport.

Planes, trains, cars, prams, they were all the same; within ten minutes of being in one she would be asleep regardless of any excitement for the destination.

That she had managed almost half an hour before the first signs of sleep grabbed her on Benjamin's jet had more to do with him and the terrifying way her heart beat when she was in his presence than it had about any fears she might have for her fiancé.

She'd had to keep her gaze fixed out of the window to stop herself from staring at him as her eyes so longed to do. When her brain had started to shut down into sleep it was images of this man flickering behind her eyes that had stopped her brain switching off completely.

Her fingers still tingled from being held in his hand, her heart still to find a normal rhythm.

Rationally, she knew there couldn't be anything too seriously wrong with Javier. Benjamin had told her Javier was unhurt and that there was nothing for her to worry about…

But there was a tension in the Frenchman now that hadn't been there before.

A prickle of unease crawled up her spine and she looked back out of the window.

When she'd last looked out of the window they

had been high above the clouds. Now the earth beckoned closer, dark shadows forming shapes that made her think of mountains and thick forests, beyond them twinkling lights, towns and cities bustling with late-evening life.

None of it looked familiar.

The unease deepened the closer to earth they flew and she kept her eyes peeled, searching for a familiar landmark, anything to counteract the tightening of her stomach and the coldness crawling over her skin.

She hardly noticed the smoothness of the landing, too busy straining through the darkness to find something familiar in the airfield they had landed in.

As she whispered words of thanks to the cabin crew and climbed down the metal stairs to the concrete ground, she inhaled deeply. Then she inhaled again.

She had been in Florence as part of her ballet company's European tour only the week before. Florence did not smell like this. Florence did not smell of lavender.

Benjamin had reached the ground before her and stood at a waiting sleek black car, the back passenger door open.

'Where are we?' she asked hesitantly, not at all liking the train of her thoughts.

'Provence.'

It took a beat for that to sink in. 'Provence as in France?'

'Oui.'

'Did I misunderstand something? I thought you said Javier was still in Florence.' Freya knew she hadn't misheard him but told herself her ears were unused to Benjamin's thick accent and therefore she must have misunderstood him.

Slowly, he shook his head. 'You heard correctly.'

Through the panicking spread of her blood she forced herself to think, to keep calm and breathe.

She had only met Benjamin once before but knew he was Javier and Luis's oldest friend. Their mothers had been best friends. They had grown up thinking themselves as family. She knew all this because of a costume fitting she'd had before Compania de Ballet de Casillas had gone on its most recent tour, the one that had taken her to the beautiful city of Florence. A new seamstress had been tasked with measuring Freya, a young, dazzlingly beautiful woman called Chloe Guillem. When Freya had casually asked if she were any relation to Benjamin, she'd learned Chloe was his sister. She should have been glad of the opportunity to speak to someone who knew Javier and taken the opportunity to learn more about her fiancé. It shamed her that she'd had to restrain herself from only asking about Chloe's brother.

'Where is he, then?'

Benjamin looked at his watch before meeting her eye again. The lights shining from his jet, which still had the engine running, made the green darker, made them flicker with a danger that clutched in her chest.

'I think he must now be in Madrid. Very soon he is going to learn you have disappeared with me. He might have already.'

'What are you talking about?' she whispered.

'I regret to tell you, *ma douce*, that I have brought you here under false pretences. Javier did not ask me to bring you to him.'

She laughed. It was a reflex sound brought about by the absurdity of what he'd just said. 'Is this a joke the pair of you have dreamt up together?'

But Javier didn't joke. She had seen no sign whatsoever that her fiancé possessed any kind of sense of humour.

Benjamin's unsmiling features showed he wasn't jesting either. The dark shadows being cast over those same features sent fresh chills racing up her spine.

The chills increased as, pulling her phone out of her bag, she saw it still wasn't working.

There was the slightest flicker in his eyes that made her say, 'Have you got something to do with my phone not working?'

'It will be reconnected tomorrow,' he said

steadily. He took a step towards her. 'Get in the car, *ma douce*. I will explain everything.'

Her heart pounding painfully, she took a step back, taking in the darkness surrounding them. High trees edged the perimeter of the huge field they had landed in, the only sound the jet's engine. The vibrant civilisation she'd glimpsed from the window could be anywhere or nowhere.

To the left of the runway sat a small concrete building, its lights on.

When Freya had exited the plane she had seen a couple of figures in high-visibility jackets walking away from them. She had to assume they'd gone into that building. She thought it safe to assume that building contained, at the very least, a working telephone.

'I'm not going anywhere else with you until you tell me what is going on,' she said in the steadiest voice she could manage while sliding her hand back into her small shoulder bag. She put her non-functioning phone back into it and groped for the can of pepper spray.

He must have seen her fear for he raised his hands, palms facing her. 'I am taking you to my home. You have my assurance that you will come to no harm.'

'No. I want to know what's going on *now*. Here. No more riddles.'

'We have much to talk about. It is better we talk in privacy and comfort.'

'And I prefer to discuss things now, before I get back on that plane and tell the pilot to take me back to Madrid.' To get to the plane, though, meant getting past *him*. A lifetime of dance had given her an agility and strength most other women didn't possess but she didn't kid herself that she had the strength to match this man, who had to be a foot taller than her own five foot five and twice her breadth.

She caught a glimmer of pity in those dangerous green eyes that made her blood chill to the same temperature as her spine.

Her fingers found the pepper spray.

She might not have the strength to match him but she would bet her life she was quicker than him.

She pulled the weapon out and aimed it at him, simultaneously stepping out of the heels that would hinder any escape. 'I *am* going back to Madrid and you can't stop me.'

Then, not giving him a chance to respond in any shape or form, Freya took off, racing barefoot over the runway and then over the dry grass to the safety that was the concrete building with its welcoming lights. Not once did she look over her shoulder, her focus solely on the door that would open and lead her to...

A locked door.

She tugged at it, she pushed it, she pulled it. It didn't budge.

'This airfield belongs to me.' Benjamin's voice carried through the still night air that was broken only by the running engine of his jet. 'No one here will help you.'

She turned her head to look back at him, surprised to find herself more angry than fearful.

Surely this was a situation where terror rather than fury should be the primary emotion?

He had lied to her and deliberately taken her to the wrong country.

No one did that unless they had bad intentions.

She should be terrified.

Benjamin hadn't moved. He stood by the car watching her impassively. For the first time she realised the car had a driver in it.

And for the first time she realised his jet's engines were still running for a reason. Not only that but it was moving...

Open-mouthed, fighting back despair, Freya watched it increase in speed down the runway.

A moment later it was in the air.

It soared into the night sky, the roar of its engines decreasing the further it flew until it was nothing but a fleeing star.

And then there was silence.

'Come with me.' This time there was no other sound but Benjamin's voice. 'You will not be touched or harmed in any way. I give you my word.'

'Why should I believe you?' she called back.

He gave what she could only describe as a Gallic shrug. 'When you get to know me, you will learn I am a man of my word.'

She shivered at words that sounded more like a threat than a promise and looked around the airfield for a route that could be her pathway to freedom. As far as she could tell they were in the middle of nowhere.

She could run. She had a good chance of making it to the perimeter before his car could catch her and then she could disappear. But where would she disappear *to*? She had no idea how far she was from civilisation, no money, a phone that didn't work…she didn't even have her shoes on.

She either took her chances and ran off into the unknown or she went with Benjamin into another unknown.

The question was which unknown held the least danger.

Benjamin watched Freya rub her arms as she stared back at him, could see her weighing up her options.

Then her spine straightened and she stepped slowly towards him, holding the spray can outwards, aimed at him.

When she was two metres from him she stopped. 'If you come within arm's reach of me I will spray this in your face. If you make any sudden movements I will spray this in your face.'

He believed her. The fear he had glimpsed before she had run had gone. Now there was nothing on her face but cool, hard resolve.

If he'd believed she was a woman to fall into a crying heap at the first sign of trouble he would never have taken this path.

Everything he had learned about her backed his instinct that Freya had grit. Seeing it first-hand pleased him. It made what had to be done easier.

'I have given you my word that you will come to no harm.'

'You have already proven yourself a liar. Your word means nothing to me.'

He turned to the open car door. 'Are you getting in or do I leave you here?' He didn't like that he'd had to lie and had swallowed back the bile his lies had produced. That bile was a mere fraction of the sourness that had churned in his guts since he'd accepted the extent of the Casillas brothers' betrayal.

She glared at him and backed into the car.

By the time Benjamin had folded himself into the back next to her, she had twisted herself against the far door, still aiming the spray can at his face.

'Don't come any closer.'

'If I wanted to hurt you I would have done so already.'

Her jaw clenched and her eyes narrowed in thought but she didn't lower her arm or relax her hold on the can. He was quite certain that if she were to spray it at him it would temporarily blind him. It would probably be painful.

'Do you always carry that thing with you?' he asked after a few minutes of loaded silence had passed while his driver navigated the dark narrow roads that led to his chateau.

'Yes.'

'Why?'

She smiled tightly. 'In case some creep tries to abduct me.'

'Have you ever used it?'

'Not in anger but there's a first time for everything.'

'Then I shall do my best not to provoke you to use it on me.'

'You can do that by telling your driver to take me to the nearest airport.'

'And how will you leave France on a commercial flight without your passport?'

Her lips clamped together at this reminder, the loathing firing from her eyes hot enough to scorch.

The car slowed over a cattle grid, the rattling motion created in the car one Benjamin never grew tired of. It was the motion of being home.

After driving a mile through his thick forest, they went over another cattle grid then stopped for the electric gates to open.

For the first time since they'd got into the car,

Freya took her eyes off his face, looking over his shoulder at the view from his window.

Her eyes widened before she blinked and looked back at him.

'You can put the spray down,' he informed her nonchalantly. 'We have arrived.'

His elderly butler greeted them in the courtyard, opening Freya's door and extending a hand to help her out.

Benjamin got out of his door in time to hear her politely say, 'Please, can you help me? I've been kidnapped. Can you call the police?'

Pierre smiled regretfully. *Je ne parle pas anglais, mademoiselle.*

'Kidnapped! Taken!' She put her wrists together, clearly trying to convey handcuffs, then when Pierre looked blankly at her, she sighed and put a hand to her ear to mimic a telephone. 'Telephone? Police? Help!'

While this delightful mime was going on, Benjamin's driver slowly drove the car out of the courtyard.

'Pierre doesn't speak English, *ma douce*,' Benjamin said. He'd inherited Pierre when he bought the chateau and hadn't had the heart to pension him off just because he spoke no other language as all other butlers seemed to do in this day and age.

She glared at him with baleful eyes. 'I'll find someone who does.'

'Good luck with that.' Only one member of his household staff spoke more than passable English and Freya had just proven she couldn't speak a word of his own language. 'Come, let us go in and get settled before we talk. You must be hungry.'

'I don't want your food.'

Turning his back to her, he walked up the terracotta steps and into the main entrance of his chateau.

'Christabel,' he called, knowing his head housekeeper wouldn't be far.

No sooner had he finished saying her name than she appeared.

'Good evening, sir,' she said in their native tongue with a smile. 'Did you have a good trip?'

'I did, thank you. Is everything well here?'

'Everything is fine and we have prepared the quarters for your guest as instructed.' Christabel's eyes flickered over his shoulder as she said this, which he guessed meant Freya had followed him inside, her bare feet muffling the usual clacking sound that could be heard when people entered the great room.

He had a sudden vision of her black high heels discarded on the runway of his airfield, a sharp pang in his chest accompanying it, which he shrugged off.

He would replace them for her.

'Thank you, Christabel. You can finish for the

evening now.' Turning to Pierre, who had also followed him in, he said, 'We require a light supper, anything Chef chooses. Bring me a White Russian and Miss Clements a gin and Slimline tonic.'

When his two members of staff had bustled off, he finally looked at his new houseguest and switched back to English. 'Do you want to talk now or would you like to freshen up first?'

She glared at him. 'I don't want to talk but, if you insist, let's get it over with because I want to go home.'

He held the mutinous black orbs in his. 'Is it not already obvious to you that you will not be going home tonight, *ma douce*?'

CHAPTER THREE

FREYA STARED INTO the green eyes that only a few hours before she had been afraid to stare too deeply at because of the strange heat gazing into them produced. Now, her only desire was to swing her small bag into his face. She'd put the pepper spray back into it and her fingers itched to take it back out and spray the entire contents at him.

'When will I be going home?' she demanded to know.

A single brow rose on his immobile face. 'That will be determined shortly. Come with me.'

'Come where?'

'Somewhere we can talk in comfort.'

He walked off before she could argue. She scowled at his retreating figure but when he went through the huge double doors and disappeared, she quickly got her own legs moving. This chateau...

She had never seen the likes of it before other than on a television screen.

Walking past sculptures and exquisite paintings, she entered another room where the ceiling was at least three times the height of a normal room, with a frescoed ceiling and opulent furniture and more exquisite works of art. She caught sight of Benjamin going through a door to the left and hurried after him. It would be too easy to get lost in this chateau, a thought amplified when she followed him through a third enormous living area, catching sight of a library—a proper, humongous, filled with probably tens of thousands of books library— on the way.

Eventually she caught up with him in yet another living area. It was hard to determine if this living area was indoors or outdoors. What should have been an external wall was missing, the ceiling held up by ornate marble pillars, opening the space to the spectacular view outside.

Her throat caught as she looked out, half in delight at the beauty of it all and half in anguish.

The chateau was high in the hills, surrounded by forests and fields that swept down before them. Far in the distance were the twinkling lights she had seen on the plane. Civilisation. Miles and miles away.

'Are you going to sit?'

She took a long breath before looking at Benjamin.

He'd sat himself on a huge L-shaped soft white sofa with a square glass coffee table in front of him.

Staring at her unsmilingly, he removed his silver tie then undid the top two buttons of his shirt.

The wrinkled old man who'd greeted them on arrival appeared as if from nowhere with two tall drinks. He placed them on the coffee table and indicated one of them to her. Then he left as unobtrusively as he had come.

Benjamin mussed his hair with a grimace then took his glass and had a long drink from it. 'What do you know about my history with the Casillas brothers?'

Surprised at his question, she eyed him warily before answering. 'I know you're old family friends.'

His jaw clenched as he nodded slowly. 'Our mothers were extremely close. They had us only three months apart. We were playmates from the cradle and it's a bond we have shared for thirty-five years. I was raised to think of Javier and Luis as cousins and I did. We have been there for each other our entire lives. You understand?'

'I guess.' She shrugged. 'Is there a point to this story?'

His eyes narrowed. 'The point to this story is the key to it.'

'You're talking in riddles again.'

'Not riddles if you would bother to listen to what I am saying to you.'

She caught the faint scent of juniper. Although only a moderate drinker—very moderate—Freya loved the refreshing coolness of a gin and tonic.

Usually she limited herself to only the one. But usually she hadn't been practically abducted. And she'd fallen asleep before she could finish the one on his jet.

And she really needed something to calm the ripples crashing in her stomach.

Giving in, she picked it up then sat on the opposite side of the sofa to him, at the furthest point she could find, using all the training that had been drilled into her from the age of three to hold her core and enable herself to be still.

Never would she betray how greatly this man unnerved her but beneath her outward stillness her pulses soared, her heart completely unable to find its usual rhythm. She wished she could put it down to fear and it unnerved her more than anything to know the only fear she was currently experiencing was of her own terrifying erratic feelings for this man rather than the situation he'd thrown her into.

She took a small sip then forced herself to look at him. 'Okay, so you grew up like cousins.'

Before he could answer the butler reappeared with a tray of food.

The tray was placed on the table and she saw a wooden board with more varieties of cheese than she'd known existed, fresh baguettes, a bowl of fruit and a smaller bowl of nuts.

'*Merci*, Pierre,' Benjamin said with a quick smile.

Pierre nodded and, just as before, disappeared.

Benjamin held a plate out to her.

'No, thank you,' she said stiffly. She would choke if she had to eat her captor's food.

He shrugged and cut himself a wedge of camembert.

'It's not good to eat cheese so late,' she said caustically.

He raised a brow, took a liberal amount of butter and spread it on the opened baguette. 'You must be hungry. I took you from the gala before the food was served. You do not have to eat the cheeses.'

'I don't have to eat anything.' She truly didn't think she could swallow anything solid, doubted her stomach would unclench enough for food until she was far from this beautiful prison.

Staring back out over the thick trees and hills casting such ominous shadows around the chateau, she resigned herself to staying under his roof for the night. As soon as the sun rose she would find something to put on her feet and leave. Sooner or later she would find civilisation and help.

He took a large bite of his baguette and chewed slowly. His impenetrable green eyes didn't move from her face.

'If you will not eat then let us continue. I was telling you about my relationship with Javier and Luis.'

Freya pushed her fears and schemes aside and concentrated. Maybe Benjamin really had gone to all this trouble to bring her here only to talk. Maybe, come the morning, his driver would take her to the airport without any fuss.

And maybe pigs could fly.

If Benjamin wanted nothing more than to talk he would have conducted this chat in Madrid.

Either way, she needed to pay attention and listen hard.

'Like cousins,' she clarified. 'A modern-day tale like *The Three Musketeers*, always there for each other.'

'*Exactemente*. Do you know the Tour Mont Blanc building in Paris?' He took a bite of creamy cheese.

'The skyscraper?' she asked uncertainly. World news was not her forte. Actually, any form of news that wasn't related to the arts passed her by. She had no interest in any of it. She only knew of Tour Mont Blanc because Sophie had been fascinated with it, saying more than once that she would love to live in one of its exclusive apartments and dine in one of its many restaurants run by Michelin-starred chefs and shop in the exclusive shopping arcade.

He swallowed as he nodded. 'You know Javier and Luis built it?'

'Yes, I knew it was theirs.'

'Did you know I invested in it?'

'No.'

'They came to me seven years ago when they were buying the land. They had a cash-flow problem and asked me to go in with them on the project as a sleeping partner. I invested twenty per cent of the asking price. When I made that first investment I was told total profits would be around half a billion euros.'

She blinked. Half a *billion*?

'It took four years for the building work to start—there was a lot of bureaucracy to get through—and a further three years to complete it. Have you been there?'

'No.'

'It is a magnificent building and a credit to the Casillas brothers' vision. Eighty per cent of the apartments were sold off-plan and we had eleven multinational companies signed up to move into the business part before the roof had been put on.'

'So it's a moneymaking factory then,' she said flatly. 'I take it there's a reason you're boring me with all this?'

The piercing look he gave her sent fresh shivers racing up her spine.

'We all knew the initial profit projections were conservative but none of us knew quite *how* conservative. Total profit so far is closer to one and a half billion euros.'

Freya didn't even know how many zeros one and a half billion was. And that was their *profit*? Her bank account barely touched three figures.

'Congratulations,' she said in the same flat tone.

It was a lot of money—more than she could ever comprehend—but it was nothing to do with her and she couldn't see why he thought it relevant to discuss it with her. She assumed he was showing off and letting her know that his wealth rivalled Javier's.

As if this chateau didn't do a good enough job flaunting his wealth!

Did he think she would be impressed?

Money was nothing to brag about. Having an enormous bank account didn't make you a better person than anyone else or mean you were granted automatic reverence by lesser mortals.

Freya had been raised by parents who were permanently on the breadline. They were the kindest, most loving parents a child could wish for and if she could live her childhood again she wouldn't swap them for anyone. Money was no substitute for love.

It was only now, as that awful disease decimated her mother's body, that she wished they'd had the means to build a nest egg for themselves. She wouldn't have felt compelled to marry Javier if they had.

But they had never had the means. They had worked their fingers to the bone to allow their only child to follow her dreams.

'I invested twenty per cent of the land fee,' Benjamin continued, ignoring her sarcasm. 'I have since invested around twenty per cent of the building costs. How much profit would you think that entitles me to?'

'How would I know?' she said stiffly. 'I'm not an accountant.'

'Take a guess.'

'Twenty per cent?'

'*Oui.* Twenty per cent. Twenty per cent investment for a twenty per cent profit. Twenty per cent of one and a half billion equals three hundred million, do you agree?'

'I'm not an accountant,' she repeated, looking away from him, her lips tightening mutinously.

'You do not need to be an accountant to agree that three hundred million euros is a lot of money.'

Her slim shoulders rose but other than a flash of colour on her high cheekbones, the mutinous expression on her face didn't change.

'I have received all of my investment back but only seventy-five million euros of the profit. The equivalent of five per cent.'

Her eyes found his stare again. 'Am I supposed to feel sorry for you?'

'You are not expected to feel anything.' Benjamin stifled his growing anger at her cold indifference. He hadn't expected anything less from the woman engaged to the coldest man in Europe. 'I am laying out the facts of the situation. Javier and Luis have ripped me off. They owe me two hundred and twenty-five million euros.'

He had earmarked that money for a charity that helped traumatised children.

The irony of why he had chosen that charity would be funny if the situation were not so damn serious. The memories of Javier and Luis's traumatisation at the death of their mother at the hands of their father had haunted him for years.

Benjamin had almost bankrupted himself investing in the Tour Mont Blanc project. He'd spent seven years clawing his way back, going higher than he had ever climbed before, investing and expanding his fine food business across the globe until he had reached the point where he didn't owe a cent to anyone. All his assets, his business and subsidiaries were his alone and could never be taken from him. Now he could do some good with the great wealth he had built for himself and Javier and Luis had stolen his first significant act from him, just as they had stolen his money, his trust and all the memories he'd held dear.

'Take it up with your lawyers.'

'I have.' Benjamin remembered the green colour Andre had turned when he'd had to tell his most lucrative client that the Casillas brothers were correct in their assertion that he was only owed five per cent of the profits.

It had been there in black and white on the contract he'd signed seven years ago, hidden in the small print. It could have been written in the largest font available and he doubted he would have noticed it back then. He had signed the contract without getting his lawyer to read it first. That was his own fault, he accepted that. It was the only contract he'd ever signed without poring over every word first. The brothers had been given until midnight to come up with the full asking price or the land would have been sold to another interested party and they would have lost the substantial deposit they'd already paid at that point.

They had come to him for help on the same day Benjamin's mother had been told there was nothing more the medical team could do to stave off the cancer ravaging her body. Although not a shock—she had not responded well to any of the treatment she'd been given—it had been the single biggest blow in his life.

Benjamin had signed with only a cursory glance at the document and transferred the money there and then. If it had been anyone else he would have refused to even contemplate the investment but it had been Javier and Luis asking. Men he regarded as kin. Men his mother had regarded as kin. Men he'd trusted unconditionally. At the time he hadn't cared that it would eat into his own cash-flow and that the chateau he'd intended to buy outright for his mother to pass the last of her days in would need him to take a hefty mortgage. It was that knock-on effect that had almost bankrupted him.

'From a legal point of view there is nothing more I can do about it.' The words felt like needles in his throat.

He'd refused to accept Andre's judgement and had fast-tracked the matter to a courtroom. The judge had reluctantly agreed with Andre.

Benjamin's rage at the situation had been enflamed when Javier and Luis successfully applied for an injunction on the reporting of the court case. They didn't want the business world to know their word was worthless or the levels to which they would stoop in the name of profit.

'Have you brought me here to tell me this thinking I will speak to Javier on your behalf?' she asked, her disbelief obvious despite the composed way she held herself.

He laughed mirthlessly and took a paring knife off the tray. He doubted very much that Javier cared for Freya's opinion. She was his beautiful prima ballerina trophy not his partner. Benjamin's hope was that her value as a trophy was greater than two hundred and twenty-five million euros.

Cutting into the peel of a fat, ripe orange, he said, 'I am afraid the situation has gone far past the point where it can be resolved by words alone.'

'Then what do you want from me? Why am I here?'

'Every action has a consequence. Javier and Luis have stolen from me and I am out of legal options.' He cut the last of the peel off the orange and dropped it into a bowl. 'In reality, the money is not important...'

She let out a delicate, disbelieving cough.

He cut into the flesh of his peeled orange. 'I am a very wealthy man, *ma douce*...'

'Well done.'

'And if it was just the money I would write it off,' he continued as if she hadn't interrupted him, cutting the orange into segments. 'But this is about much more than money, more than you could understand. I am not willing to let it go or let them get away with it. You are my last bargaining chip.'

'Me?' For the first time since she had entered his home, her composure made an almost imperceptible slip. 'But I had nothing to do with it. I was still in ballet school when you signed that contract.'

'*Oui.* You.' He looked at his watch and smiled. 'In three minutes it will be midnight. In three minutes Javier will receive a message giving him exactly twenty-four hours to pay the money owed.'

She swallowed. 'Or...?'

'If the Casillas brothers refuse to pay what they have taken from me then by the laws of natural justice I shall take from them, starting with you. If they do not pay then, *ma douce*, the message Javier will receive any moment tells him his engagement to you will be over and that you will marry me instead.'

CHAPTER FOUR

THE BURN THAT had enflamed Freya's brain earlier returned with a vengeance. She gazed into the resolute green eyes that gave nothing away and felt her stomach clench into a pinpoint.

Freya had no illusions about her lack of intellect. Ballet had been her all-consuming passion since she could walk. She couldn't remember a time in her life when she hadn't breathed dance and her education had suffered for it. She had one traditional educational qualification and that was in art.

But this didn't mean she was stupid and she would have to be the dimmest person to walk the earth not to look into those green eyes and recognise that Benjamin was deadly serious.

This was revenge in its purest form and she was his weapon of choice to gain it.

She was his hostage.

Her kidnapper stared at her without an ounce of pity, waiting for her response to his bombshell.

She responded by using the only means she had at her disposal, *her* only weapon. Her body.

Jumping up from the sofa, she swept an arm over

the coffee table, scattering the crockery and glasses on it, but didn't hang around to see the damage, already racing through the non-existent wall and out into the warm grounds. Benjamin's surprised curse echoed behind her.

Security lights came on, putting a spotlight on her but she didn't care. She would outrun them. She dived into the thick, high shrubbery that she hoped surrounded the perimeter of the chateau and hoped gave adequate camouflage until she found the driveway they had travelled to reach the chateau and which she would follow until she found the road.

She had run from Benjamin earlier. She had reluctantly gone back to him because she had thought he was the unknown that posed the least danger.

She had made the wrong choice. Her heated responses to his physicality, the strange chemical responses that set off inside her every time she looked into his green eyes had stopped her recognising the very real danger she was in.

How big was this chateau and its grounds? she wondered desperately as she cut her way through the trees and hedges, trusting her sense of direction that she was headed the right way.

It seemed to take for ever before she peered through the shrubbery to find the courtyard Benjamin's driver had dropped them off at. The night was dark but there were enough ground lights for her to see the electric gates they had driven through.

Quickly she looked around it and saw the gate, a high wrought-iron contraption with spikes at the top that linked the high stone wall she would have to scale if she were to get away.

Keeping to the shadows, Freya treaded her way to the wall, her heart sinking the closer she got.

It was at least twice her height.

She stepped cautiously from the high tree she'd hidden behind for a better look. The wall was old. It had plenty of grooves and nooks for her to use to lever herself up. If she kept to the shadows she'd be able to scale it away from the estate lights…but then she wouldn't be able to see what was on the other side if she were in the dark.

Determination filled her. If she didn't climb this wall she would never escape.

She took one deep inhalation for luck then darted forward.

The moment she stepped off the thick, springy ground of the woods and onto the gravelled concrete, it seemed as if a thousand lights suddenly shone on her.

Not prepared to waste a second, she raced to the wall, found her first finger holes and began to climb.

She'd made it only two feet off the ground when she heard shouts. Aware of heavy footsteps nearing her, she sped up. The top of the wall was almost within reach when she stretched to grip a slightly protruding stone and, too late, realised it was loose.

With a terrified scream, she lost her hold entirely and fell back, would have crashed to the ground and almost certainly landed flat on her back had a pair of strong arms not been there to catch her as assuredly as any of her dance partners would have done.

Instinct had her throw her arms around Benjamin's neck while he made one quick shift of position to hold her more securely.

She squeezed her eyes shut and tried her hardest to open her airwaves.

She couldn't breathe. The shock of the fall and the unexpected landing had pushed all the air from her lungs. But her terrified heart was racing at triple time, tremors raging through her body.

How had he reached her so quickly? He must have run at superhuman speed.

'Do you have a death wish?'

His angry words cut through the shock and she opened her eyes to find his face inches from her own, furious green eyes boring into hers.

He was holding her as securely as a groom about to cross the threshold with his new bride but staring at her with all the tenderness of a lion about to bite into the neck of its prey.

Then he muttered something unintelligible under his breath and set off back to the chateau.

'You can put me down now,' she said, then immediately wished she hadn't spoken as now that she could breathe again she could smell again too. Her face was so close to Benjamin's neck she could smell the muskiness of his skin under the spicy cologne.

He shook his head grimly.

She struggled against him. 'I'm quite capable of walking.'

His hold tightened. 'And have you run away and put yourself in danger again?'

'I won't—'

'What were you thinking?' he demanded. His footsteps crunched over the gravel. 'If I hadn't been there to catch you...'

'What did you expect?' Her words came in short, ragged gasps. The feel of his muscular body pressed so tightly against her own made her wish he were made of steel on the outside as well as the inside. Damn him. If he were a robot or machine she could ignore that he was human and that her body was behaving in the opposite manner that it should to be held in his arms like this.

Her lips should not tingle and try to crane closer to the strained tendons on his neck, not to bite but to kiss...

'I expected you to listen, not run into the night. The forests around the chateau are miles deep. You can spend days—weeks—lost in them and not meet a soul.'

'I don't care. You can't kidnap me and hold me to ransom and think I'm going to just accept it.' She squeezed her eyes shut to block his neck from her sight.

If only she could block the rest of him out too.

God, she could hardly breathe for fear and fury and that awful, awful awareness of him.

Pierre had the door open for them. As Benjamin carried Freya over the threshold, the butler saw her feet and winced.

Benjamin sighed inwardly before depositing her onto the nearest armchair and instructing Pierre, who really should have long gone to bed, to bring him a bowl of warm water and a first-aid kit.

'Telling him to bring handcuffs so you can chain me in your horrible house?' his unwilling guest asked snidely.

'That's a tempting idea, but no.' Tempting for a whole host of reasons he refused to allow himself to think of.

Holding Freya in his arms like that had felt too damn good. The awareness he'd felt for her from that first look had become like an infection inside him.

He must not forget who she was. Javier's fiancée. His only possible means of getting his money back and giving Javier a taste of the betrayal he himself was feeling.

Kneeling before her, he took her left foot in his hand. She made to kick out but his hold was too firm. 'I am not going to hurt you.'

'You said that before,' she snapped.

'The harm you have caused to your feet is self-inflicted. Keep still. I want to look for damage.'

The full lips pulled in on themselves, her black eyes staring at him maleficently before she turned her face to the wall. He took it as tacit agreement for him to examine her feet. The foot in his hands was filthy from walking bare through all the trees and shrubbery but there was no damage he could see. He placed it down more gently than she deserved and picked up her right foot. It hadn't fared so well. Tiny droplets of blood oozed out where she'd trodden on something sharp.

Pierre came into the room with the equipment he'd requested, along with fresh towels.

'Going to do a spot of waterboarding?' she asked with a glare.

He returned it with a glare of his own. 'Stop giving me ideas. I'm going to clean your feet…'

'I can clean my own feet…'

'And make sure you have no thorns or stones stuck in them.'

'You're a doctor?'

'Only a man with a sister who could never remember to put shoes on when she was a child.' And rarely as a teenager either. Chloe had moved out of the chateau a few years ago and he still missed her lively presence in his daily life.

His much younger sister was as furious with the Casillas brothers as he was and had insisted on helping that night. He'd given her the task of delaying Luis from the gala and she had risen to it with aplomb. Now she was safely tucked up in first class flying to the Caribbean to escape the fall-out.

'I'm a dancer,' Freya said obstinately. 'My feet are tough.'

'Tough enough to risk infection? Tough enough to risk your career?'

'Being held hostage is a risk to my career.'

'Stop being so melodramatic. You are not a hostage.' He took a sterile cloth and dipped it in the water, squeezing it first before carefully rubbing it against the sole of her foot.

'If I'm not allowed to leave that makes me a hostage. If I'm being held for ransom that makes me a hostage.'

'Hardly. All I require is twenty-four hours of your time. One day.' He rubbed an antiseptic wipe to the tiny wounds at the sole of her foot, then carefully placed it down on its heel.

'And what happens then? What if Javier says no and refuses to pay?'

'You have doubts?' He lifted her other foot onto

his lap. 'Are you afraid his love for you is not worth such a large amount of money?'

She didn't answer.

Raising his gaze from her feet to her face, he noted the strain of her clenched jaw.

'You are the most exciting dancer to have emerged in Europe since his mother died. You have the potential to be *the* best and Javier is not a man who settles for second best in anything. You are not publicity hungry. You will give him beautiful babies. You tick every box he has made in his list of wants for a wife. Why would he let you go?' As he spoke he cleaned her foot, taking great care in case there were any thorns hidden in the hard soles not visible to the naked eye.

Freya's assessment of her feet being tough was correct, the soles hard and calloused, the big toe on her right foot blackened by bruising.

His heart made a strange tugging motion to imagine the agonies she must go through dancing night after night on toes that must be in perpetual pain. These were feet that had been abused by its owner in a never-ending quest for dance perfection. And what perfection it was…

Benjamin had been dragged across the world in his younger years by his mother, who had been Clara Casillas's personal seamstress as well as her closest friend. His childhood home had been a virtual shrine to the ballet but he'd been oblivious to it all, his interest in ballet less than zero. He'd thought himself immune to any of the supposed beauty the dance had to offer. That had been until he'd watched a clip of Freya dancing as Sleeping Beauty on the Internet the other week.

There had been something in the way she moved when she danced that had made his throat tighten and the hairs on his arms lift. He'd watched only a minute of that clip before turning it off. He'd tried to rid his mind of the images that seemed to have etched themselves in his brain ever since.

Freya belonged to his enemy. He had no business imagining her.

And yet...

As hard as he had tried, he had been completely unable to stop his mind drifting to her or stop the poker-like stabs of jealousy to imagine her in Javier's arms that had engulfed him since he'd first set eyes on her.

'Javier knows I am a man of my word,' he continued, looking beyond the battered soles of her feet to the smooth, almost delicate ankles and calves that were undeniably feminine. A strange itch started in his fingers to stroke the skin to feel if it was as smooth to his touch as to his eye. 'He knows if I say I will marry you then I will marry you.'

'You've rigged everything to fall your way but unless you have something even more nefarious up your sleeve you can't marry me without my permission.' Steel laced her calm voice. 'Besides, you said I only have to stay with you for one day—you've given me your word too. You are lying to one of us. Which is it?'

'I have not lied to either of you. Have you not wondered *why* I had your phone tampered with?'

Clarity rang from her eyes. 'To stop me warning him. You don't want me in a position to scupper your plans by telling him the truth.'

He smiled. She was an astute woman. 'Javier will know by now that we left the gala together. I do not doubt he will hear we left hand in hand. He will know you left willingly with me and will be wondering how deep your involvement goes. If he trusts and loves you he will know you are my pawn and will pay me my money to get you back. If he doesn't trust or love you enough he will refuse to pay and cut you adrift. If he cuts you adrift the ball rolls into your court, *ma douce*. The moment Javier reaches his decision, whatever that decision may be, you will be free to leave my chateau without hindrance. If you choose to leave I will fly you back to Madrid even if your choice is to plead your case with him and throw yourself at his mercy. If, however, you decide to stick with a certainty then you can marry me. I am willing to marry you on the same terms you were going to marry him—I assume there was a pre-nuptial agreement. I am prepared to honour it. Or you can decide to have nothing to do with either of us and get on with your life.'

Benjamin put the towel down by the now cold bowl of water and got to his feet. 'Whatever happens, I cannot lose. Javier will pay for what he has done one way or another.'

While he'd been speaking, Freya's silent fury had grown. He'd seen it vibrate through her clenched fists and shuddering chest, the colour slashing her cheeks deepening.

Finally she spoke, her words strangled. 'How can you be so cruel?'

'A man reaps what he sows.'

'No, I meant how can you be so cruel to *me*? What have *I* done to merit this? You don't even know me.'

'You chose to betroth yourself to a man without a conscience. I notice you have accepted at face value that Javier and Luis stole from me. You know the kind of man he is yet still you chose to marry him. What kind of woman does that make you?'

The colour on her face turned an even deeper shade of red, her stare filled with such loathing it was as if she'd stored and condensed all the hatred in the world to fire at him through eyes that had become obsidian.

She rose from her seat with a grace that took his breath away. 'You don't know anything about me and you never will. You're the most despicable excuse for a human being I have ever met. I hope Javier calls your bluff and calls the police. I hope he gets a SWAT team sent in to rescue me.'

He reached out to brush a thumb against her cheekbone. It was the lightest of touches but enough for a thrill to race through him at the silky fineness of her skin.

He sensed the same thrill race through her too, the tiniest of jolts before the eyes that had been firing at him widened and her frame became so still she could be carved from marble.

'If he were to involve the police the news would leak out and his deception would become public knowledge,' he murmured, fighting the impulse to run his hand over her hair and pull the tight bun out, imagining the effect of that glorious hair spilling over her shoulders like a waterfall. 'But the police would not do anything even if he did go to them because I have not broken any law, just as Javier has not technically broken any law.'

'You kidnapped me.'

'How? You got into my jet and my car of your own free will.'

'Only because you lied to me.'

'That was regrettable but necessary. If lying is a crime then the onus would be on you to prove it.'

'You paid someone to disconnect my phone.'

'Again, the onus would be on you to prove it.'

Her throat moved before her voice dropped so

low he had to strain to hear. 'How do you sleep at night?'

'Very well, thank you, because my conscience is clear.' Finally he moved his hand away and took a step back from her lest the urge to taste those tempting lips overcame him. 'I will get a member of staff to show you to your quarters. Sleep well, *ma douce*. I have a feeling tomorrow is going to be a long day for both of us.'

Then he half bowed and walked away.

CHAPTER FIVE

FREYA PACED HER bedroom feeling much like a caged tiger prowling for escape. The only difference between her and the tiger was she hadn't been locked in. She could walk out right now and never look back. Except it was now the early hours of the morning and her feet would rightly kill her if she tried to escape again. Third time lucky, perhaps? A third attempt to escape into the black canopy of Benjamin's thick forest? She might even emerge on the other side alive.

She slumped onto the bed with a loud sigh and propped her chin on her hands. Her feet stung, the corset of her dress dug into her ribs and she was suddenly weary from her lack of food. The pretty pyjamas on her pillow looked increasingly tempting.

A young maid had shown her to her quarters. She hadn't spoken any English but had been perfectly able to convey that the pyjamas were for Freya and that the clothes hanging in the adjoining dressing room were for her too. There were even three pairs of shoes to choose from, all of them worse than ballet slippers for an escape in the forest.

All the clothes were Freya's exact size, right down to the underwear. She guessed Benjamin's sister had passed on her measurements.

The planning he must have undertaken to get her there made her shiver.

He was remorseless. Relentless. He left nothing to chance, going as far as installing a camera outside her bedroom door. She'd seen the flashing red light and known exactly what it was there for. A warning that should she attempt to leave her quarters she would be seen in an instant. If she found a landline phone she would never get the chance to use it.

Without laying a finger on her he'd penned her in his home more effectively than a collie rounding up sheep.

But he *had* touched her.

The shivers turned into tingles that spread up her spine and low in her abdomen as she remembered how it had felt to have his large, warm hands holding her feet so securely, different tingles flushing over her cheek where he had brushed his thumb against it.

She had never met a more unrepentantly cruel person in her life and being part of the ballet world that was saying something.

But he had cleaned and tended to her feet with

a gentleness that had taken her breath away. She had expected him to recoil at them—anyone who wasn't a dancer would—but instead she'd detected a glimmer of sympathy. Bruised, aching feet were a fact of her life. Smile through the pain, use it to drive you on to perfection.

She had to give him his due—in that one respect Benjamin had been the perfect gentleman. If she'd allowed any of her straight male colleagues to clean her feet she could only imagine the bawdiness of their comments. The opportunity for a quick grope would have been almost impossible for them to resist. The ballet world was a passionate hotbed, the intimacy of dancing so closely together setting off hormones that most didn't want to deny let alone bother to fight. Freya wasn't immune to it. The passion lived in her blood as it did in everyone else's; the difference was when the music stopped the passion within her stopped too. She had never danced with a man and wanted the romance to continue when the orchestra finished playing. She had never felt a man's touch and experienced a yearning within her for him to touch her some more.

Benjamin had held and touched her feet and she had had to root her bottom to the chair so as not to betray her own body's betrayal of wanting those long fingers to stop tending and start caressing. She had had to fight her own senses to block out the thickening of her blood at his touch, had fought to keep the detachment she had spent a lifetime developing.

She squeezed her eyes shut, her brain-burn deepening at how she reacted so physically to the man who threatened to ruin *everything*.

She was caught in a feud between two men—three if she counted Luis—but it wasn't Freya who had the potential for the greatest suffering as a consequence of it, it was her mother. Her mother was the only reason she had agreed to Javier's emotionless proposal.

You know the kind of man he is yet still you chose to marry him. What kind of woman does that make you...?

It made her a desperate one.

Dance was all she knew, all she was, her life, her soul, her comfort. She had achieved so much from her humble beginnings but there was still so much to strive for, both for herself and for her parents who had made so many sacrifices to get her where she was today. Imagining the pride on their faces if she were to get top billing at the Royal Opera House or the Bolshoi or the Metropolitan gave her all the boost she needed on the days when her feet and calves seared with such pain that she forgot why she loved what she did so much.

Javier's proposal had given her hope. He would give her all the space she needed to be the very best. Marriage to him meant that if she did make it as far as she dreamed in her career then she would have the means to fly her parents all over the world to watch her perform. Much more importantly, her mother would have the means to be alive and well enough to watch her perform, not be crippled in pain with the morphine barely making a dent in the agony her body was putting her through.

But she *did* know the kind of man Javier was and that was why she had no faith he would pay Benjamin the money he owed. She didn't doubt he and Luis owed Benjamin money, although how they could have got one over the French billionaire she could not begin to guess, and right then she didn't have the strength to care.

Her forthcoming marriage was nothing more than a marriage of convenience. Javier's feelings for her ran no deeper than hers did for him.

If he didn't pay Benjamin then it meant their marriage was off. It meant no more money to pay for her mother's miracle drugs.

If he didn't pay it meant she would have to trust the word of the man who'd stolen her and hope he'd been telling the truth that he would marry her on the same terms.

Because if Javier didn't pay she would have to marry Benjamin. If she didn't her mother would be dead by Christmas.

* * *

Benjamin was on his second cup of coffee when a shadow filled the doorway of the breakfast room. He'd drained the cup before Freya finally stepped inside, back straight, chin jutted outwards, dressed in three-quarter-length white jeans and a dusky pink shirt, her glorious hair scraped back in another tight bun.

The simplicity of her clothing, all selected by his sister, did not detract in the least from her graceful bearing, and Benjamin found himself straightening and his heart accelerating as she glided towards him.

She allowed Christabel, who had followed her in, to usher her into the seat opposite his own and made the simple act of sitting down look like an art form.

'Coffee?' his housekeeper asked as she fussed over her.

'Just orange juice, thank you,' she answered quietly.

Only when they were alone did Freya look at him.

He'd thought he'd become accustomed to the dense blackness of her eyes but right then the weight of her stare seemed to pierce through him. He shifted in his seat, unsettled but momentarily trapped in a gaze that seemed to have the ability to reach inside him and touch his soul...

He blinked the unexpected and wholly ridiculous thought away and flashed his teeth at her. 'Did you get any sleep?'

She smiled tightly but made no verbal response.

'You look tired.'

She shrugged and reached for her juice.

'Have some coffee. It will help you wake up.'

'I rarely drink caffeine.'

'More for me then.' He poured himself another cup as the maid brought Freya's breakfast tray in and placed it in front of her.

His houseguest gazed at the bowls before her in surprise then smiled at the maid. It was a smile that made her eyes shine and for a moment Benjamin wished he were the one on the receiving end of it.

'Please thank the chef for me,' she said. 'This is perfect. She must have gone to a great deal of trouble.'

As the maid didn't speak English, Benjamin translated.

The moment they were alone again, Freya said, 'Has Javier been in touch?'

'Not yet.' He'd turned his phone's settings so only Javier, Luis and Chloe could reach him. He didn't want any other distractions.

She closed her eyes and took a long breath. He could see her centring herself in that incredible way he had never seen anyone else do, as if she were swallowing all her emotions down and locking them away. If he hadn't seen those bursts of anger-fuelled adrenaline when she had run away at his airfield and then when she had sent his supper flying before fleeing into the night, he could believe this woman never lost her composure.

And yet for all her stillness there was something about her that made her more vivid than any other woman he had ever met, a glow that drew the eye like a breathing, walking, talking sculpture.

What kind of a lover she would be? Did she burn under the sheets or keep that cloak of composure?

Had her exotic, intoxicating presence turned his old friend's heart as well as his loins? Had he lost himself in her...?

Benjamin shoved the thought away and swallowed back the rancid taste forming in his mouth.

He should be hoping Javier *had* lost himself in her arms as that would make it more likely for him to pay to get her back. He should not feel nauseous at the thought of them together.

That sick feeling only became more violent to think of Freya losing herself in Javier's arms.

How deeply did her feelings for Javier run?

If they had any depth then why did her eyes pulse whenever she looked at *him*?

He inhaled deeply, trying to clear his mind. He needed to concentrate on the forthcoming hours until Javier made his move. Only then could he decide what his own move would be.

In that spirit, he looked pointedly at the varying bowls of food his chef had prepared for her. He'd sent Christabel to check on his unwilling houseguest earlier and see what, if anything, she required for breakfast. He did not deny his relief to learn she'd abandoned her short hunger strike.

'What are you having?' he asked. 'It looks like animal feed.'

'Granola. Your chef has kindly made it fresh for me.'

'Granola?'

'Rolled oats.'

'Animal feed.'

She pulled a face at him and placed a heaped spoonful of berries on her animal feed, following them with a spoonful of almonds. Then she spooned some natural yogurt onto it and stirred it all together. As she raised the spoon to her mouth she paused. 'Do you have to watch?'

The colour staining her cheeks intrigued him. 'It bothers you?'

'You staring at me? Yes.'

'Why?'

'Because...' Freya put the spoon back in the bowl. She could hardly believe how self-conscious she felt sitting before him like this. She spent hours every day with her every move scrutinised by choreographers, fellow dancers, audiences and had long ago learned to tune out the weight of their stares.

Yet sitting here with Benjamin's swirling green eyes fixed upon her she was aware of her body in ways she had never been before, could feel the blood pumping through her, heating with each cycle.

It wasn't merely herself and the components of her own body that she was freshly aware of, it was Benjamin too, this Lucifer in disguise. The vibrating hairs on her nape and arms strained towards him as if seeking his scent and the heat of his skin, her senses more alert than they had ever been before.

'It just does,' she said tightly. 'Why don't you get yourself something to eat and leave me in peace?'

'I rarely eat in the morning,' he informed her.

'Cheese late at night then no breakfast…all the ingredients for health problems when you reach middle age.'

A glimmer came into his eyes. 'I can assure you I am in peak physical health.'

She could see that for herself though she would never admit it to him and felt a pang of envy at a life where you could eat any morsel you liked without scrutiny and without having to weigh up its nutritional value or energy-boosting properties.

Oh, to have the freedom to eat whatever you liked—or not—whenever you liked…

Benjamin's phone suddenly buzzed loudly.

She met his narrowed green eyes the moment before he reached for it.

'It's an email from Javier,' he said matter-of-factly.

Her stomach dropped. 'Already?'

He nodded. 'He has sent a copy to your email too.'

'What does it say?'

He studied it for a long time before sliding the phone to her.

The email contained no text. Javier had sent an attachment of two adjoining photos.

She blinked a number of times before the pictures she was staring at came into focus and their significance made itself clear.

They had been taken by one of the photographers at the gala who had spotted something intriguing about them leaving together and decided to capture it. The first shot caught the moment when they had paused in the hotel lobby for Benjamin to briefly explain the situation, the other had them walking out of the hotel hand in hand.

It was the first picture she found herself unable to look away from and, she knew in the pit of her stomach, it was the reason Javier had sent the pictures to her too.

Benjamin's face had been mostly obscured but her own features were there for all to see, and all could see her black eyes staring intently into his and her body tilting towards him. They looked like a pair of lovers caught in the midst of a most intimate conversation.

The blood whooshed up and into her brain.

That look in her eyes as she'd stared at him…

Had she really looked at Benjamin like that?

She covered her mouth, horrified.

She couldn't even bring herself to say anything when Benjamin's large hand stretched across the table to take his phone back from her.

Freya was so shamed and mortified at the expression captured on her face she feared her vocal cords had been stunned into silence for ever.

Nothing was said between them until another loud buzzing cut through the silence, a continuous buzz signalling a phone call.

Benjamin put it on speakerphone.

His eyes rested on Freya as the gravelly Spanish tones of Javier Casillas filled the room.

'You will not receive a cent from me, you son-of-a-bitch. Keep her. She's all yours.'

Then the line went dead.

This time the silence between them was loud enough for Freya to hear the beats of her thundering heart.

The room began to spin around her, the high ceiling lowering, the wide walls narrowing.

She was going to be sick.

She might very well have *been* sick had the most outrageous sound she'd ever heard not brought her sharply back to herself and the room back into focus.

Benjamin, his eyes not once dropping their hold on hers, was laughing.

'How can you think this is funny?' she asked with a croak, dredging the words from the back of her throat. 'You've lost.'

And she had lost too. Javier had emailed the pictures to her too as a message. Their engagement was over.

'Lost?' Benjamin's face creased with mirth. He threw his head back, his laughter coming in great booms that echoed around her ears. 'No, *ma douce*, I have not lost. I told you last night, I cannot lose.'

It was a struggle to breathe. 'He's not going to pay the money.'

'There was only an evens chance that he would. There were only two end scenarios: Javier would pay or he would not. This result is not my preferred one but I can take satisfaction that he will be burning with humiliation at the photographs of us so it is not a loss by any means.'

'Not a loss for you, maybe, but what about me? He's never going to take me back. You know that, right? These pictures make it look like I was encouraging you...that I was a part of it.'

Oh, God, that look in her eyes as she'd stared into his...

There was not an ounce of penitence to be found

in his glittering eyes. 'You don't have to lose anything, *ma douce*. Your career is safe. You are one of the most exciting dancers in the world. If Javier is foolish enough to sack you then I guarantee another company will snatch you up.'

'You think I care only about my career?' she demanded.

His laugh was merciless. 'My sister says you are the most driven dancer she has ever met, but if it is the loss of your fiancé that grieves you then I suggest you have a rethink. If he had feelings for you he would have fought for you. If he'd believed in your love he would have fought for you. You should be thanking me. I am saving you from a lifetime of misery.'

'I can assure you, you are not. I told you last night that you don't know anything about me.'

'If he means that much to you, now is your chance to go to him and plead your case,' he said sardonically. 'He has made his choice, which means you are now free to make yours. Say the word and I will arrange transportation to take you back to Madrid. You can be back there by lunch.'

Rising from her chair, Freya leaned forward to eyeball him. She had never known she could feel such hate for someone. Her heart was beating so frantically against her ribcage she had to fight to get the words out. 'Believe me, my preferred outcome would be to leave this awful excuse for a home and never have to see your hateful face again. Quite frankly, if I were stuck on a desert island with the choice between you and a rat for company, the rodent would win every time.'

Something flickered on his darkly handsome face, the smug satisfaction vanishing.

A charge passed between them, so tangible she felt it pierce into her chest and thump into her erratic heart.

He gazed at her with eyes that swirled and pulsed before his lips curved into a knowing smile and he too leaned forward. 'The way you were looking at me in that photograph proves the lie in that.'

CHAPTER SIX

'I DON'T KNOW what you're talking about.' Freya hated that her burning cheeks contradicted her.

Benjamin rose slowly from his seat and walked around the table to her, that feline grace she had seen before taking a dangerous hue, the panther stalking towards its prey.

She twisted around so her thighs pressed into the hard wood, her usually nimble feet becoming like sludge.

And then he was standing in front of her, that strong neck her lips kept longing to press into right there in her eye line, standing close enough for his fresh spicy scent to seep into her senses.

'I think you know exactly what I'm talking about, *ma douce.*' He placed a hand on the arch of her neck and dropped his voice to a murmur. The feel of his fingers on her skin burned through her, the heat from his breath catching the loose strands of her hair and carrying through it to her scalp and down into her bloodstream. 'The camera never lies. Javier saw the desire you feel for me. I have seen it too and I have *felt* it, when I carried you back into my home and the moonlight shone on us both. You say you hate me but still you long for my kiss.'

Freya found herself too scared to move. Too scared to breathe. Terrified to make the slightest twist in her body lest her lips inch themselves forward to brush against the warm neck so close to her mouth and the rest of her body, aching at the remembrance of being held so securely in his arms, press itself wantonly against him.

Focus, Freya. The next few minutes will determine you and your mother's whole futures.

He moved a little closer so his breath danced over the top of her ear, electrifying parts inside her she hadn't known were there. 'There is an attraction between us that has been there since we first saw each other in Javier's garden.'

She gave a tiny shake of her head to deny his words but he dragged his hand from her neck and placed a finger on her lips, standing back a little so he could stare straight into her eyes.

'Now you no longer belong to him, we are free to act on it.' Benjamin brushed the finger from her lips to rest lightly on her cheek. She truly had the softest skin he had ever touched, more velvet than flesh.

He'd always known it would be fifty-fifty whether Javier would pay up, which was why he had gone to the lengths he had to make sure that whatever the outcome, he would still win.

He hadn't expected the destruction of Javier and Freya's relationship to feel like a victory that would taste as sweet as if Javier had paid in full.

Never again would he be haunted by thoughts of Freya enjoying herself in his enemy's bed because she had been correct that Javier would never take her back. She could plead with him but Benjamin knew Javier too well. His Spanish foe's reputation and pride were the fuel he needed to get through the day. In one stroke Benjamin had battered them both and soon he would set his sights on Luis too.

Benjamin was well aware the actions he'd taken made him as bad as the men he sought to destroy but he didn't care. Why should he? Who had ever cared for him?

His mother had loved him but when he had discovered the Casillas brothers' treachery the past had come back into sharp focus and he'd been forced to accept that her love for him had always been tied with her love for them. Louise Guillem had loved Javier and Luis as if they were children of her blood because, for his mother, Clara Casillas had been the love of her life. A platonic love, it was true, but with the emotional intensity of the most heightened love affair. Benjamin had been a by-product of that love, a child to raise alongside Clara's, not wanted as a child should be for himself but more as a pet, an accessory.

His father had long gone, leaving the marital

home when Louise had fallen pregnant by accident a decade after Benjamin had been born. Already fed up playing second fiddle to the World's Greatest Dancer, his father had refused to hang around and raise a second accessory. Benjamin had never missed him—you had to know someone to miss them and he had never properly known his father—but, again, with the past being brought back into focus, he had realised for the first time that his father hadn't just left his mother but his only son too. He hadn't cared enough to keep their tentative relationship going.

Then there was Javier and Luis. Their betrayal had been the most wrenching of all because it had made him look at the past with new, different eyes and reassess all the relationships he had taken for granted and unbury his head from the truth.

The only relationship he had left was with his sister but she was a free spirit with wounds of her own, a beautiful violin with broken strings.

Every other person he'd trusted and cared for had used or betrayed him.

He was damned if he would trust or care again.

This beautiful woman with eyes a man could fall into was no innocent. He regretted that he'd had to use her but it had been a necessary evil. He would not regret destroying her relationship with Javier. If she had cared an ounce for his foe she would not be staring at him as if she wanted him to devour her.

Dieu, a man really could fall into those eyes and never resurface…

But there was something else breaking free in the heady depths of those eyes, a fire, a determination that made him drop his hand from her cheek and step back so he could study her carefully without her sultry scent playing under his nose and filtering through into his bloodstream…

The moment he stepped away she folded her arms across her chest and seemed to grow before his eyes.

'The only thing we're going to act on is your word.' Freya's husky voice had the same fiery determination as resonated in her eyes.

'You are ready to be taken back to Madrid?'

This time she was the one to laugh, a short, bitter sound. 'Yes. But not yet. Not until you have married me.'

For a moment it felt as if he had stepped onto quicksand.

He shook his head. 'You want to marry me?'

'No. I would rather marry the rodent on the desert island but you told me I would have three choices once Javier had made his. He won't take me back, not even if I get down on my knees and beg. I need the money set out in our pre-nuptial agreement so going back to Madrid and resuming my single life is not an option either, which leaves just one remaining choice—marrying you. You need to honour the contract Javier and I signed on our engagement as you said you would.'

He stared into her unsmiling face, an unexpected frisson racing up his spine.

Marriage to Freya…?

He had made his threat to Javier with the full intention of acting on it if it came to it but never had he believed she would go along with it, let alone demand it of him.

He tried to envisage Javier's reaction when he heard the news but all he could imagine was Freya naked in his bed, the fantasies he'd been suppressing for two months suddenly springing to life in a riot of erotic colour.

Marriage had never been on his agenda before. He'd spent the past seven years so busy clawing his business back to health and then into the business stratosphere that any thoughts of wedlock had been put on the back burner, something to be considered when his business no longer consumed his every waking thought.

Now the thought of marriage curdled his stomach. Marriage involved love and trust, two things he was no longer capable of and no longer believed in.

'Were you lying to me when you gave me your word?' she challenged into the silence.

'I save the lies for your ex-fiancé. He's the expert at them. And I am thinking you must be good at them too seeing as you fooled him into believing you had feelings for him.'

'I didn't fool or lie to anyone. Javier and I both knew exactly what we were signing up for.'

'You admit you were marrying him for his money?'

'Yes. I need that money.'

'And what did Javier get out of marrying you other than a prima ballerina on his arm?'

Fresh colour stained her cheeks but her gaze didn't flicker. 'The contract we signed spells it out. If you're the man of your word you say you are, you will duplicate it and honour it.'

'You are serious about this?'

'Deadly serious. The ballet company is on a two-week shutdown. I was supposed to marry Javier next Saturday. I presume with all the strings you're able to pull you can arrange for us to marry then instead. Either that or you can pay me now all the money I would have received from Javier, say, for the first ten years of our marriage.' Her eyes brightened, this idea clearly only just occurring to her. 'That can be my compensation for being the unwitting victim in your vindictive game. It comes to…' her brow furrowed as she mentally calculated the sum '…around twenty million. I'll be happy to accept half that. Call it ten million and I go back to my life and we never have to see each other again.'

'You want me to pay you off?' he asked, part in astonishment and part in admiration.

'That would be the best outcome for both of us, don't you think?'

He shook his head slowly, intrigued and not a little aroused at the spirit and fight she was showing. No wonder Javier had chosen her for his wife. She was magnificent. '*Non, ma douce*, the choice was marriage or nothing. If I pay you off, I get nothing from it.'

'Your conscience will thank you.'

'I told you before, my conscience allows me to sleep well. With you in my bed every night I will be able to sleep even more sweetly.' His arousal deepened to imagine that wonderful hair fanned over his pillow, the obsidian eyes currently firing fury at him firing only desire…

'Maybe you should read the contract before assuming I will be in your bed every night. You might find you prefer to pay me off.'

'Unlikely but, even if that is the case, the knowledge Javier will spend the rest of his life knowing it is my ring you wear on your finger and not his will soften the blow.'

'You really are a vindictive monster, aren't you?'

'You insult me and speak of my conscience when you are a self-confessed gold-digger.' He smiled and closed the gap that had formed between them and placed a hand on her slender hip. There was no danger of trusting or caring for this woman, even if he was capable of it and even if she did have eyes he could sink into. 'We don't have to like each other to be good together…and I think we could be *very* good together. Marry me and you have everything you would have had if you had married Javier.'

'And you get continued revenge,' she finished for him, her tone contemptuous.

'*Exactemente.* We *both* get what we want.'

Freya could smell the warmth of his skin beneath the freshness of his cologne…

Benjamin was *not* what she wanted. He provoked her in ways Javier never had. Javier was scary but Benjamin terrified her for all the wrong reasons.

She wouldn't be swapping one rich man for another, she would be swapping ice for fire, safety for danger, all the things she had never wanted, all the things she had shied away from since she had learned sex was the only control she had over her body.

There was not a part of her external body that hadn't been touched or manhandled; a grab of her arm to raise it an inch higher, rough hands on her hips to twist her into the desired shape, a chuck under the chin to lift it, partners holding her intimately in dance… Her external body was not hers; it belonged to dance. Her body was public property but her emotions and everything inside her belonged to herself.

That the control she'd worked so hard for was in danger of slipping for this man, this vindictive, abhorrent…

She clamped her lips together to contain a gasp.

Benjamin had taken another step closer. Their bodies were almost flush.

For the first time in her life someone had hold of her hip and she could *feel* it, inside and out, her blood heating and thickening to treacle.

She closed her eyes and breathed in deeply, trying to block her dancing senses and contain what was happening within her frame.

'You know what this means?' he murmured.

She swallowed and managed a shake of her head.

'It means you and I are now betrothed. Which means we need to seal the deal.'

Before she could guess what he meant, he'd hooked an arm around her waist and pulled her tight against him. Before she could protest or make any protective move of her own, he'd covered her mouth with his.

Having no preparation or warning, Freya found herself flailing against him, her hands grabbing his arms as her already overloaded senses careered into terrifying yet exciting new directions. She struggled helplessly to keep possession of herself while his lips moved against hers in what she instinctively knew was the final marker in the game he'd been playing, Benjamin claiming her as his in an expert and ruthless manner that...

His tongue swept into her mouth and suddenly she didn't care that it was all a game to him. Her body took possession of her brain for the very first time and she was kissing him back, taking the dark heat of his kisses and revelling in the sensation they were evoking in her. Such glorious, heady sensations, burning her skin beneath her clothes, sensitising flesh that had only come alive before for dance. She loosened her hands to wind them around his neck and press herself closer still while he swept his hands over her back, holding her tightly, possessively, devouring her mouth as if she were the food he needed to sustain himself. When his hand moved down to clasp her bottom and grind their groins together, it was *her* moan that echoed between them.

Her breasts were crushed against his chest, alive and sensitised for the first time in her life, making her want to weep that she had chosen to wear a bra when she so rarely bothered, and as these thoughts flickered in her hazy mind reality crashed back down.

All the clothes she wore, her underwear, her shoes, every item designated as hers under this roof had been bought without her knowledge.

She was a pawn in Benjamin's game of vengeance and she *hated* him.

She would not accept his kisses with anything but contempt.

When Freya suddenly pulled out of his arms and jumped back, seeming to leap backwards through the air yet still making the perfect dancer's landing, Benjamin had to blink rapidly to regain his focus and sense of place.

What the hell had just happened?

Breathing heavily, he stared at her, stunned that one simple kiss could explode like that. He'd known the attraction between them was strong but that… that had blown his mind.

He hadn't experienced such heady, evocative feelings from a kiss since…since ever, not even those illicit teenage kisses when he'd first discovered that the opposite sex was good for something more than merciless teasing.

She stared back, eyes wide and wary, her own breaths coming in shallow gulps, her cheeks flushed. Her hair was still pulled back in that tight bun but there was something dishevelled about her now that made the heavy weight in his loins deepen.

He put a hand on the table, partly to steady himself and partly to stop himself crossing the room to haul her back into his arms. His loins felt as if they had been set on fire, the burn spread throughout him but concentrated there, an ache such as he had never experienced before that threatened to engulf his mind along with the rest of him.

Had she reacted to Javier's kisses with that same intensity…?

The thought deflated the lust riding through him as effectively as a pin in a balloon.

He needed air.

'Your pre-nuptial agreement. Where is it?' he asked roughly.

A flash of confusion flittered over her features before she blinked sharply. 'In Javier's safe but I have a copy of it on an email attachment.'

'*Bien.* I will get your phone unlocked. When it is working again, forward it to me. I will get it re-drafted with both our names on it. It will be ready to sign by the end of the day.'

CHAPTER SEVEN

BENJAMIN RAPPED LOUDLY on the door to Freya's quarters, his heart making as much noise in his chest as his knuckles made on the door.

It was incredible to think these would be her permanent quarters.

When he had bought the chateau seven years ago there had been a vague image of a future Madame Guillem to share the vast home and land with but it had been a secondary image. He'd bought it for his mother and, at the time, nursing her through her final months had been his only concern. Not long after her funeral, he'd found himself unable to repay the mortgage and forced to face the reality of his financial situation. Nursing his mother had taken him away from his business. The bills had mounted. Suppliers had threatened court action. He'd been days away from losing everything.

All thoughts of a future Madame Guillem had been buried. He'd dated. He'd had fun. But nothing permanent and definitely nothing serious. He'd had neither the physical time nor the mental space to make a relationship work.

It was only when he'd reached a position in his life where he could take his foot off the accelerator and slow things down enough for a real life of his own that he'd reached the inescapable conclusion that he would never trust anyone enough to pledge his life to them. As much as he'd regretted it would likely mean he would never have children, another of those vague in-the-future notions, he would not put himself through it. If he couldn't trust the people he'd loved all his life how could he trust a stranger?

He didn't have that worry with Freya. Knowing there was no trust to fake made taking this step more palatable.

Reading through the contract she and Javier had signed had made it even more so.

He had read it, shaking his head with incredulity at what it contained.

He could easily see his old friend signing this cold, emotionless contract but for the hot-blooded woman whose kisses had turned him to fire to sign such a thing stretched the realms of credulity.

But then, she was already proving to be far more fiery a woman than he'd thought Javier would commit himself to.

He hadn't seen her since their explosive kiss that morning. He'd been busy in his office organising things. She'd kept herself busy doing her own thing, his staff keeping discreet tabs on her.

He knocked again. After waiting another thirty seconds, he pushed the door open and let himself in.

Her quarters were large and comfortable, a small reception area leading to a bedroom, bathroom and dressing room to the left, and a spacious living area to the right, where the faint trace of music played out through the closed door. He opened it and paused before stepping over the threshold.

All the furniture had been pushed against the far wall to create a large empty space. The music came from her freshly working phone.

Freya had contorted herself into the strangest shape he'd ever seen the human body take right in the centre of the room. Her calves and knees were on the carpet as if she'd knelt to pray but instead of clasping her hands before her and leaning forward, she'd gone backwards into a bridge, her flat stomach arched in the air, her elbows on the floor where her toes rested, her face in the soles of her bare feet with her hands clasping both her heels and her temples.

It looked the most uncomfortable pose a person could manipulate themselves into but she didn't appear to be in any discomfort. If anything, she seemed at peace, her chest expanding and her stomach softening in long, steady breaths.

He found his own breath stuck in his lungs. He

didn't dare make a sound, afraid that to disturb her would cause her to injure herself.

After what felt like hours but in reality was probably less than a minute she uncoiled herself, walking her hands away from her feet then using them to push herself upright.

Kneeling, she finally looked at him. She showed no concern or surprise at his appearance in her quarters.

He'd been so entranced with what he'd seen that it was only when her eyes met his that he noticed all she had on were a black vest and a pair of black knickers.

If she was perturbed that he had walked into her quarters while she had hardly any clothes on she didn't show it.

But then, recalling all the years spent touring with Clara Casillas, he had never met a body-shy ballerina before. He'd seen more naked women in the first ten years of his life than if he'd been raised in a brothel. It was a fact of their life. Freya was a woman who spent her life with her body under a microscope, different hands touching it for different reasons, whether to lift, to shape or to dress.

Desire coiled through his loins to imagine what it would feel like to lift this woman into his arms as a lover…

He would bet she had poise and grace even when she slept and felt a thickening in his loins to know it wouldn't be long before he discovered that for himself.

And, as his imagination suddenly went rampant with heady thoughts of this beautiful, supple woman in his bed, those long, lithe legs wrapped around him, those black eyes currently staring at him without any expression coming alive with desire, the strangest thing of all occurred. Freya blushed.

She must have felt the heat crawling over her face for her features tightened before she jumped gracefully to her feet, going from kneeling to standing in the time it took a mortal to blink.

'If you'll excuse me, I'll put some clothes on,' she said stiffly.

The lump in his throat prevented him from doing more than stepping aside to let her pass through the door to her bedroom.

Breathing deeply, he took a seat on the armchair while he waited for her to return, keeping his thoughts and imagination far away from sex, trying to quell the ache burning in his loins.

They had business to take care of.

Feeling more together in himself when she came back into the living room, he said, 'What were you doing?'

She'd put her three-quarter-length white jeans back on and covered her chest with an off-the-shoulder navy top. Her battered feet were bare.

She sat on the leather sofa nestled next to his and twisted her body round to face him. 'Yoga. That pose was the Kapotasana.'

'It sounds as painful as it looks.'

The glimmer of a smile twitched on her lips. 'It's invigorating and, under the circumstances, necessary.'

'Why?'

'I need to keep fit. I'm used to dancing and working out for a minimum of seven hours a day. I need to keep my fitness levels maintained, I need to stretch and practise regularly or it will be extra hard when I return to the studio. This is all I have available to me…unless you have a secret dance studio tucked away somewhere with a barre?'

'I am afraid not but you are welcome to use my gym and swimming pools and sauna. There's tennis courts too.'

She pulled her lips in together. 'I have to be careful using a gym and swimming. It's what they do to my muscles—they bulk them in all the wrong places. I've never played tennis before and wouldn't want to risk taking it up without advice.'

He looked around again at the space she had created for herself in this room and knew without having to ask that this was not suitable for her to practise dancing in.

'Still, I'm sure you're not here to discuss my fitness regime,' she said, changing the subject and straightening her back before nodding at the file in his hand. 'Is that the contract?'

He'd almost forgotten what he had come here for.

Pulling his mind back to attention, he took the sheets of paper out of the folder. 'I've booked our wedding for Thursday.'

She was silent for beat. 'Thursday?'

'Oui.'

'I was supposed to marry Javier on Saturday.'

'At this short notice there are no slots available for Saturday.'

'Couldn't you have bribed or blackmailed someone?'

'I pulled enough strings to bypass the notice period. If it's a Saturday wedding you long for we can always wait a few weeks.' He stared hard at her as he said this. Having now read the terms of the contract he understood why she was keen to marry on the same day she would have married Javier. On the day of their wedding he would transfer two hundred thousand euros into her account, the first recurring monthly payment of that sum. According to the contract, Javier had already paid her two lump sums of one hundred thousand euros.

'No,' she declined so hurriedly he could see the euro signs ringing in her eyes. 'Thursday is fine.'

He gave a tight smile. 'I thought so. I will take you to the town hall tomorrow to meet the mayor and fill out some forms but the arrangements are all in hand. Is your passport in your apartment?'

She nodded. 'I've spoken to my flatmate. She's got it safe.'

'I will send a courier to collect it.'

'I'll go and get it. I need to collect the rest of my stuff.'

'Your possessions can be couriered over with the passport.'

'I want to get them myself.'

The thought of her being in the same city as Javier set his teeth on edge. '*Impossible*. There is too much to arrange here.'

'I need my clothes.'

'I have appointments in Paris after our meeting with the mayor tomorrow. You can fly there with me and buy whatever you need.'

'With what? Fresh air? I can't buy an entire new wardrobe with one hundred and fifty euros, which is all I have in my account.'

His lips curved in distaste. 'You have spent all the money Javier has already given to you?'

'Yes. I had…'

'I have no cares for what you spend your money on. I will give you a credit card. Buy whatever you need with it. Consider it an early wedding present. While you are there you can buy a wedding dress.'

'Something black to match your heart?' she suggested with a touch of bitterness.

'You are hardly in a position to talk of my heart when you were party to a contract like this one.'

There was the slightest flinch. 'Javier and I drew up a marriage agreement that suited us both.'

'It does not suit me.'

'You said you would honour it.'

'And I will. I have only changed one item.'

'I'm not signing unless it's the original with only Javier's name substituted for yours.'

'You will if you still want the fortune and all the assets that come with it.'

'What have you changed?'

'Look for yourself.' He handed the file to her. 'The change is highlighted in red.'

She took it from him with a scowl.

'May I remind you,' he said as she flicked through the papers, 'that it is your choice to marry me. I am not forcing your hand.'

She didn't look up from the papers. 'There was no other choice for me.'

'The lure of all that money too strong to give up?' he mocked.

But she didn't answer, suddenly looking up at him with wide eyes, colour blasting over her cheeks. 'Of all the things you could have changed, you changed *that*?'

'I am not signing away a chunk of my fortune and my freedom to spend only one night a week in a bed with my wife.' He'd read that part of the long, detailed pre-nuptial agreement with his mouth open, shaking his head with disbelief as he'd wondered what kind of a woman would sign such a document.

Scheduled, mandated sex?

And then he had read the next section and his incredulity had grown.

How could the woman who kissed as if she were made of lava agree to such a marriage?

He stared at Freya now and wondered what was going on in that complex brain. She was impossible to fathom, a living contradiction. Scalding hot on the outside but seemingly cold on the inside. Which was the real Freya: the hot or the cold one?

'I will comply in full with the rest of the contract but when we are under the same roof we sleep in the same bed. If it is not something you can live with I suggest you tell me now so I can make the necessary arrangements for your departure from my home.'

Freya stared into eyes as uncompromising as his words and dug her bruised toes into the carpet. Her skin itched with the need for movement, the hour of yoga she had done before he had walked into her quarters nowhere near enough to quell the fears and emotions pummelling her.

Their kiss...

It had frazzled all her nerve endings.

How could she have reacted to his kiss like that? To *him*?

It had been her first proper kiss and it had been everything a first kiss should be and, terrifyingly, so much more.

She had spent the day searching for a way to purge her heightened emotions but her usual method of dancing her fears away was not available to her. She'd taken a long walk through his grounds and explored the vast chateau praying that somewhere within the huge rooms would be one she could use to dance in. It had been like Goldilocks searching for the perfect porridge and bed but without the outcome; not one of the rooms had been right. The majority could work with their proportions but the flooring was all wrong, either too slippery or covered in carpet, neither of which were suitable and could be dangerous.

Meditation and yoga were her fail-safe fallbacks, clearing her mind and keeping her body limber, but they weren't enough, not for here and now when she was as frightened for her future and as terrified of what was happening inside her as she had ever been.

Her brain burned to imagine Benjamin's private reaction when he had read the section that covered intimacy in her pre-nup. Javier had insisted it be put in, just as he had insisted on the majority of all the other clauses, including the one stating they would only have a child at a time of Freya's choosing. He hadn't wanted them to ever get to a point in the future where either could accuse the other of going back on what had been agreed. That agreement would always be there, a guide for them to enter matrimony and ensure a long, harmonious union without any unpleasant arguments or mis-understandings.

The whole document read as cold and passion-less, entirely appropriate for a marriage that had nothing to do with love but business and safety.

Javier had been cold but he *had* been safe. There had never been any emotional danger in marry-ing him.

She had never had to dig her toes into the ground when she was with him. There had been no physi-cal effect whatsoever.

The brain burn deepened as she read the con-tents again, the only change being Benjamin's name listed as Party One. And the new clause stating they would share a bed when under the same roof.

Her heart thumped wildly, panic rabid and hot inside her.

When she had envisaged making love to Javier it had been with an analytical head, a box to tick in a marriage that would keep her mother alive and ease her suffering for months, hopefully years, to come.

There was nothing analytical about her imag-inings of Benjamin. She had felt something move inside her in that first look they had shared, a flare of heat that had warmed her in ways she didn't understand and could never have explained.

Their kiss had done more than warm her. She could still feel the scorch of his lips on hers and his taste on her tongue. Meditation and yoga had done nothing to rid it but it had helped to a small extent, allowing her to control her raging heart and breathing when he had unexpectedly entered her quarters.

And then he had stared at her with the look that suggested he wanted to strip the last of her clothing off.

She had never been shy skimpily dressed in front of anyone before but in that moment and under the weight of that look she had felt naked for the first time in her life.

And she was expected to share his bed and give herself to this man who frightened her far more than her ice-cold fiancé ever had?

He, Benjamin, was her fiancé now...

She could do this, she assured herself, breathing deeply. She had faced far scarier prospects, like when she'd been eleven and had left the safety and comfort of her parents' home to become a boarder at ballet school. That had been truly terrifying even though it had also been everything she'd wanted.

Joining the school and discovering just how different she'd been to all the other girls had almost had her begging to go home. Having been accepted on a full scholarship that included boarding fees, she'd been the only girl there from a poor background. In comparison, all the others had been born with silver spoons in their mouths. They'd spoken beautifully, worn clothes that hadn't come from second-hand stores and had had holiday homes. Freya's parents hadn't even owned the flat they'd lived in.

Somehow she had got through the chronic homesickness and the merciless taunts that nowadays would be considered bullying by burying herself in ballet. She had learned to hide her emotions and express it all through dance, fuelling the talent and love for ballet she had been lucky enough to be born with.

If she could get through that then she was equal to this, equal to Benjamin and the heady, powerful emotions he evoked in her. She could keep them contained. She must.

She could not predict what her future held but she knew what the consequences would be if she allowed this one clause to scupper their marriage plans: a slow, cripplingly painful death for her mother. She would do anything to ease her mother's suffering. Anything. The first message that had popped into her phone when it had come back to life earlier was her father's daily update. Her mother had had 'a relatively comfortable night'. Translated, that meant the pain had only woken her a couple of times.

'If you're allowed to make a change in the contract then I must be allowed to make one too,' she told him, jutting her chin out and refusing to wilt under the swirling green eyes boring into her. She would not let him browbeat her before they had even signed the contract.

'Which is?'

'I was supposed to be moving in with Javier. My flatmate's already found a new tenant to take my room so I'm not going to have anywhere to live when I'm at work. I want you to buy me an apartment to live in in Madrid. We're on a two-week shutdown so that's plenty of time for a man of your talents to buy one for me.'

She saw the faintest clenching of his jaw before his eyes narrowed.

'I will not have my wife working for my rival.'

'The contract states in black and white that I continue my career for as long as I like and I do what is best for me and my career. You have no say and no influence in it.'

'I can change the terms to include that.'

'You said one change. Or have you forgotten you're a man of your word?'

No, he had not forgotten, Benjamin thought grimly. It had simply not occurred to him that, having agreed to marry him, Freya would want to return to Madrid. She could work anywhere. It didn't have to be there.

'He will make your life a misery,' he warned.

'Javier has nothing to do with the day-to-day running of the company. He's rarely there.'

But Madrid was his home. The thought of Freya living in the same city as *him* set his teeth further on edge.

'There are many fine ballet companies in France who would love to employ you. I will never interfere with your career but in this instance I am going to have to insist.'

'Insist that I quit Compania de Ballet de Casillas?'

'Oui.'

The black eyes shot fire-dipped arrows at him. 'So you want to punish me and an entire ballet company for the sins of its owners, is that what you're saying?'

'Non. I am saying I do not wish for my wife to work for her ex-lover. It is not an unreasonable request.'

Something shone in her eyes that he didn't recognise, a shimmer in the midst of her loathing that disappeared as quickly as it had appeared. 'It's a request now? That's funny because the word *insist* made it sound remarkably like a demand.'

'This will be my only interference.'

Her foot tapped on the carpet but her tone remained calm. 'So I can get a job working in Japan and you won't complain?'

'You can work wherever you like.' As long as it was far from the Spaniard who had captured her long before he'd set eyes on her...

'Just not for Javier.'

'Just not for Javier.'

She sucked in a long draw of breath before inclining her head. 'I will hand my notice in but I will work my notice period. You can add that to the contract and reiterate you are never to interfere with my career.'

'How long is your notice period?'

'Two months. That will allow me to do the opening night of the new theatre. I'm on all the advertising literature for it. I can't pull out. It's the biggest show of my life. I've worked too hard to throw it away.'

'D'accord.' He took in his own breath. Two months was nothing. He could handle her working for Javier for that period.

He reminded himself that until that morning he had expected her to insist on returning to Madrid.

'You share my bed when we are under the same roof and hand your notice in to Compania de Ballet de Casillas. I buy you a property to live in while you work your notice and guarantee never to interfere with your career again. I believe that is everything unless there was something else you wished to discuss.'

Colour rose up her cheeks, her lips tightening before she gave a sharp nod. 'Just one thing I think it is best to make clear. I may be agreeing to share a bed with you but that does not mean you take ownership of my body. It belongs to me.'

'I think the kiss we shared earlier proves the lie in that, *ma douce*,' he said silkily.

The chemistry between them was real, in the air they both inhaled, a living thing swirling like a cloud, shrouding them.

'Think what you like.' She dropped her gaze. 'I will not be your possession.'

'I am not Javier. I do not expect you to be. But I do expect a wedding night. After that, you can turn your back to me as often as you wish. I do not forget the clause in the contract allowing Javier to take a mistress without question or explanation and, seeing as you have not requested that clause to be removed, it stands for me too. And as you know, I am a man who likes to have all options on the table.'

Her nostrils flared as she jutted her chin back out again, a sign he was starting to recognise meant she was straining to keep her composure.

Let her try and keep it. Come their wedding night he would shatter that composure and discover for himself if her veins ran hot or cold.

CHAPTER EIGHT

'YOU BOUGHT EVERYTHING you need?' Benjamin asked as his helicopter lifted into the air to fly them back to Provence after what had proven to be an extremely long day. 'It doesn't look like much.'

They had sorted out the paperwork for their wedding first thing then flown to Paris. Having work to do, he'd arranged for his PA's assistant who spoke English to take Freya shopping.

He had been so consumed in recent months with his feud with the Casillas brothers that he'd neglected his business. He'd hardly stepped through the headquarters of Guillem Foods in weeks and knew from bitter experience how dangerous it could be to take his eye off the ball. Now that the first part of his revenge had been extracted he needed to concentrate on his business for a while before making his next move. Luis would have to wait.

Yet even though he'd needed his brain to engage with Guillem Foods, he'd had to fight to keep his attention on the job because his mind kept wandering back to the woman who would be his wife in three days' time.

What was it about Freya that consumed his thoughts so much? She'd lodged herself in his mind from that first look, a fascination that had refused to shift that, now she was under his roof, was turning into an obsession.

Things would be better once he'd bedded her. The thrill of the chase and the unknown would be over and she would become mere flesh and bone.

He stared at her now, convinced she was the perfect wife for him. When the desire currently consuming him withered to nothing she would not care. Her own desire for him, unwanted as it was to her, wouldn't last either. Her heart was too cold for lust to turn into anything more. The marriage agreement she had willingly signed giving herself to two separate men proved that.

Freya was a gold-digger in its purest form. A gold-digger who at some point in the future would give him a child...

A sudden picture came into his head of Freya dancing, a miniature Freya at her feet copying her moves; the child they would have together, the child that would make the chateau he had bought for his mother to end her days in a home.

It was a picture he had never imagined with anyone in all his thirty-five years and the strength of it set blood pumping into his head and perspiration breaking out over his skin.

So powerful was his reaction to the image that

it took a few moments to realise she was answering his question.

'Sophie's packing my stuff up for me. I've arranged for the courier to collect it later when he gets my passport.

'Will you not need it for your new apartment in Madrid?' How he hated to think of her returning there but a deal was a deal. The contract had been signed over breakfast.

He'd already instructed an employee to hunt for a suitable home in Madrid for her. The main stipulation was that it be located as far from the district Javier called home as possible.

'I'll decide what to take with me when I go back,' she said. 'It'll be mostly my training stuff I take.'

'Would it not be easier to have separate wardrobes for each home?' He spent the majority of the year in his chateau but had apartments in Paris and London and houses in Australia, Argentina and Chile. Each had its own complete wardrobe, allowing him to travel lightly and spontaneously when the need or mood arose.

She shrugged, not looking at him. 'That would be wasteful.'

Incredulous, he stared at her. 'You're going to have two hundred thousand euros credited to your account every month for the rest of your life on top of your earnings and you are worried about being wasteful?'

The black eyes found his.

His heart thumped in the unnerving way it always seemed to do whenever those eyes captured his.

'I learned not to waste things as a child.'

'You had strict parents?'

'No, I had poor parents.' She said it matter-of-factly but with a hint of defiance and more than a little hint of pride.

'How poor?' Sob-stories of childhoods were everywhere. Some were even genuine.

However much he might despise the Casillas brothers Benjamin would never deny how traumatic their childhood had been. It made his own seem like one of the fairy tales Freya danced to.

'So poor that when I was offered a full scholarship to the ballet school with boarding fees included, they *had* to let me board as they couldn't afford the commuting fees.'

'Did the scholarship not include travelling fees?'

'Only for me, not for them. Commuting would also have meant one of them would have had to give up one of their jobs to get me there and back twice a day and they were on the breadline as it was. They didn't think it was safe for me to travel from one side of London to the other on my own.'

'How old were you when you went to boarding school?'

'Eleven.'

Benjamin winced. That was a horribly young

age to leave home. 'Were they those awful pushy parents we read so much about nowadays?'

Her eyes glinted with anger. 'No. They were wonderful. They held down two jobs each and juggled things so one of them was always home with me. They worked their backsides off to pay for my ballet lessons when I was little and then to support me at ballet school because the full scholarship didn't cover everything. They did it because they loved me and wanted me to be happy.'

'Ballet makes you happy?' It might have sounded like a stupid question but he remembered from his early childhood on tour with Clara Casillas the haunted faces of some of the dancers who had definitely not been happy with their lives.

'More than anything else. It's my life.'

He studied her in silence, their gazes fixed on each other.

He had never felt the pull of a woman's eyes the way he did with Freya. It was like staring into a black pool of unimaginable depths.

'Do you want to invite your parents to the wedding?' Their marriage had such a surreal quality to it that the thought she might want the people she loved there had never occurred to him until that moment.

'They don't travel.'

'Were they not going to come to your wedding to Javier?'

She shook her head.

'Have you told them?'

'That I've exchanged fiancés like a child swapping marbles in the playground? Yes, I spoke to my dad about it this morning. I told him you had stolen me.' The faintest smile curved on her lips. 'At least it wasn't a lie. How he interpreted it is up to him.'

'How did he take it?'

'I told you, my parents only want what's best for me. They love me and want me to be happy. Are you going to invite anyone?'

'The only person I would want is my sister but she is away.' Chloe was still in the Caribbean, taking advantage of the ballet company's shutdown for a well-deserved holiday and an escape from the fall-out.

Javier's representatives had issued a short statement that morning saying that his engagement to Freya Clements was over. No details had been provided and the press were in a spasm of speculation, the main question being whether Freya's disappearing act with Benjamin at the gala had been the cause.

'No other family to ask?' she asked.

'You are interested in me?'

'Not in the slightest. I'm merely curious as to what I'm marrying into.'

'My mother died seven years ago. My father and I are not close and never have been.' Not even when they had lived under the same roof. His mother had raised him as if she were a single parent and his father had let her, never suggesting that their only son stay behind with him rather than tour the ballet world. A second unplanned pregnancy ten years after the first had been the final nail in his parents' precarious marriage.

He'd barely noticed when his father left, let alone missed him.

'Are you sure you don't want to have anyone there?' he pressed. 'There is not much time if you do.'

'I would have said Sophie but she told me earlier that she's going to make the most of the shutdown and go off somewhere. I suppose it saves her being put in a compromising position.'

'Because she works for Compania de Ballet de Casillas?'

'Like all ballet companies it's a hotbed of gossip.'

'Then don't go back,' he stated immediately, seizing the advantage.

'Do you really think I could care less what my colleagues think of me?' she asked coolly. 'Sophie is the only one I care about. We've been friends since ballet school.'

'A long friendship then,' he observed. Not many friendships survived childhood. He'd thought those that did were the strongest. He'd learned the hard way how wrong that notion was.

'The only time we've been apart since we were eleven was when I first moved to Madrid.'

'She followed you there?'

She shrugged and turned her face to the window. Soon they would be landing back in Provence, time speeding on. 'There were vacancies for new dancers to join the *corps de ballet*. I put in a good word for her. She's the only dancer I'm close to. The others can say what they like about me, it doesn't matter in the slightest, but I will not have Sophie hurt.'

He stared at her shrewdly, nodding his head slowly. 'I can see why Javier thought you were the ideal woman for him to marry. Neither of you invite closeness. But you seem to have loyalty, which he does not possess. And there is fire in your veins, *ma douce*. There is passion. I have seen it and I have felt it. What I find myself wondering is if *he* ever saw it or if it was something you kept hidden from him.'

'How very poetic.' If not for the quiver in her voice and the tapping of her foot, he could believe the drollness of her tone was genuine.

'It is no matter.' He leaned forward. 'In three nights' time I will discover for myself how deep the fire runs inside you.'

Freya's eyes were just reaching that heavy about-to-fall-asleep stage when the motion of the car driving over the cattle grid pulled her back to alertness. She stared out of the window her forehead was pressed against; the forest that marked Benjamin's territory overhung and surrounded them, the moonlight casting shadows that made her shiver. This was a fairytale forest where the nightmares came out at night.

The prickling of her skin told her Benjamin, beside her in the back of the car, was watching her.

He was always watching her. As much as she wished she could claim differently, her eyes always sought his too.

It was the night before their wedding. The intervening days had been relatively easy to handle as he had spent them in Paris or in his office working. She had occupied herself as much as she could, taking long walks in the forest that scared her so much at night but which during the day came alive with wildlife and glorious colours. But there was nowhere to dance, not a single room within the multitude where she could risk putting pointe shoes on and letting her body relax in the movement that had always invigorated and comforted her.

The evenings were the hardest.

They dined together but the dishes they were served were entirely separate. Benjamin favoured dishes like juicy steaks and creamy mashed potato while she ignored the tantalising aromas and concentrated on her super-salads and grilled chicken, the meals punctuated by periodic polite conversation.

It was all the unspoken conversations that had her feet tapping and her limbs aching for movement, when their eyes would lock together and electricity would flow between them, so thick she felt the currents in her veins. She could never finish her meals fast enough to escape to the sanctuary of her quarters where, mercifully, he had not attempted to join her again.

If he did, she was no longer confined to practising yoga in her underwear; all her leotards and practice outfits had been delivered from Madrid with her passport and neatly put away.

She kept her passport on her at all times.

That night he had taken her out to the theatre to watch a play she couldn't remember the plot of, the movements and words on the stage passing her by in a blur, her concentration focused solely on the man sitting in the private box beside her.

'We are home,' he said quietly as the chateau appeared before them, illuminated in its magnificence.

'This is not my home.' Her denial was automatic.

'This will be our main marital house and the base for which we lead our lives. I want it to feel like home for you but you need to be the one to make it that. Do whatever you feel is necessary.'

Unable to help herself, she turned to look at him.

She wanted to deny his words more vehemently. She wanted to throw it all in his face, tell him that she could never make a home in the place he had basically imprisoned her in but she couldn't get the words out. The expression in his eyes had frozen her tongue to the roof of her mouth.

She had seen desire there; it was always there. She had seen loathing, she had even glimpsed pity in those green depths, but this...

This look made her insides melt into liquid and her heart race into a thrum.

This was a look of possession but not the look of a buyer appreciating his chattel. It was the possessive way a man looked at his lover, and the thought made the liquid in her insides *burn* to think that, in only one night, she would *be* his lover.

He was telling her to treat his home as her own and, more than that, he *meant it*. She could see it in the eyes she found herself continually seeking.

She could never imagine Javier saying something like that. Their engagement party had been nothing but an exercise in showing her off to his peers—he didn't have friends, he had acquaintances—and cementing their forthcoming union. She had never felt comfortable in his home and he had never done or said anything to make her feel that she should feel comfortable there. In truth, she had dreaded moving into that villa and living within the cold, emotionless walls.

Yet for all her dread at marrying him, she'd felt safe. He could touch her but he could never hurt her.

Benjamin on the other hand...

'Do you want a drink?' he asked casually as she hurried through the chateau doors. 'A last drink to celebrate the last night of our freedom?'

'No, thank you.' She shook her head for emphasis. 'I'm going up. I need to do some yoga and get some sleep.'

'Yoga at this time of night?'

She took the first step up the cantilevered stairs. 'If I can't dance it's the next best thing.'

And God knew she needed to do something. She would be marrying this man in fourteen hours.

'In that case, *bonne nuit*.'

Not looking back and holding the rail tightly, she skipped up the stairs feeling his stare on her with every step she took.

She had to remember that Benjamin had stolen her. He had *stolen* her.

Nothing he did or said could make up for that.

Marrying him was the only way she could salvage the mess that he had created for her in his ruthless game of revenge.

If she dropped her guard, he had the potential to hurt her in ways she did not have the imagination to imagine.

The wedding ceremony was simple and, best of all, quick.

Two hours after they had been pronounced husband and wife, they sat alone in an exclusive restaurant at the pretty little town they had married in, and all Freya could remember of the ceremony itself was how she'd trembled; her hands, her voice as she'd made her vows, but she could remember nothing of the vows themselves. She remembered how warm her skin had been and how certain she'd been that the mayor, who'd officiated the service, and the witnesses he'd brought in could all hear the hammering of her heart.

She couldn't remember the faces of the witnesses. She couldn't remember the face of the photographer who had taken the official picture of the newly married couple on the steps of the town hall but she could remember the butterflies that had let loose in her stomach as she'd waited for the kiss that would show the world she belonged to Benjamin, striking a further blow to the pride of the man she should have married.

She had held her core tightly in dread and anticipation. Benjamin had stared intently into her eyes but instead of stamping his possession on her mouth, had pulled her to him so her cheek pressed against his chest and his chin rested on the top of her head. She could remember the scent of his cologne and the warmth of his skin through the smart suit he'd married her in, and most vividly she remembered the dive of disappointment that the kiss she'd worked herself up for had never happened.

From that day the world would know her as Freya Guillem. It would be her professional name, just as she had agreed to take Javier's name what now felt a lifetime ago.

She could no longer remember Javier's face. She didn't think she had ever looked at it properly.

But she knew every contour of Benjamin's. His features had been committed to her memory all those months ago in that one, long, lingering look when she should never have noticed him in the first place. Her hungry eyes had soaked in all the little details since she had been living under his roof and now she knew the exact position of the scar above his lip, the differing shades of his eyes depending on the light and his mood, the unruliness of his black eyebrows if he didn't smooth them down, the faint dimple that appeared in his left cheek when he smiled, which wasn't often.

But when he did smile…

His smile had the capacity to make her stomach melt into a puddle.

Trying her hardest to hide the fresh tremors in her hand, she took another drink of her champagne and readily allowed the maître d' to refill it.

'Is the food not to your liking, madam?' he asked, staring with concern at her plate.

'It's delicious,' she replied honestly. 'I'm just not very hungry.'

She'd had to virtually force-feed herself the few

bites she'd had of her challans duck with crispy pear and other little morsels of taste sensation artfully displayed on her plate.

The town they'd married in was a beautiful place of old, steep, narrow streets and chic, impeccably dressed men and women. This was rural France but with a modern twist, its eclectic shops and restaurants catering to the filthy rich. The restaurant Benjamin had taken her to to celebrate their nuptials was the plushest of the lot, its chef the recipient of so many awards he was a household name, even to her. Benjamin had hired the whole restaurant for their exclusive use.

'Has anticipation caused you to lose your appetite?' the man she had married only a few hours before asked with a gleam in his eyes, the look of seduction, the unspoken promise that the kiss he had failed to deliver on at the top of the town hall steps would soon be forthcoming.

Whatever had affected her appetite had not had the same effect on him, she thought resentfully, staring at his cleared plate. He had eaten with the same relish he ate all his meals. Apart from breakfast, she remembered. Benjamin had an aversion to breakfast.

'Anticipation about what?' she challenged. 'If you think I'm nervous about sharing a bed with you then I'm afraid I must disappoint you.'

And she wasn't nervous. She was terrified.

The gleam in his eyes only deepened. 'I don't think it is possible that you could disappoint me, *ma douce.*'

You'll be disappointed when you discover my complete lack of experience.

She knew she should tell him. It was something she had told herself repeatedly these past few days but every time she practised in her head what to say, her brain would burn and she'd get a queasy roiling in her belly. Benjamin was expecting to share his bed with an experienced woman, not a virgin.

Would he laugh at her? Or simply disbelieve her? Maybe he would even refuse to sleep with her, a thought that would have sent her into hysterical laughter if her vocal cords hadn't frozen. As if he would care. The man was remorseless.

Whatever his reaction would be she had yet to find the words to tell him and now the time was speeding up and all she could do was drag this meal out for as long as she could to delay what she knew was inevitable.

Yet staring into those green eyes that gazed so blatantly back at her, she couldn't deny there was truth in Benjamin's observation. Anticipation had laced itself within her fear. It had steadily coiled itself through her bloodstream and now she didn't know if it was fear or anticipation that had her clutched in its grip the strongest.

She had to get a hold on herself and keep her head. Keep her control, the only part of herself that would be left for herself when this night was over.

He reached over to take her hand, leaning forward as he rubbed his thumb against her wrist to stare at her with a piercing look that sent fresh tingles racing through her blood. She was certain he must be able to feel the pulse behind the skin of her wrist throbbing madly.

His voice dropped to a sensuous murmur. 'As you are not hungry for food...' He raised her hand and pressed his lips to the very spot on her wrist his thumb had brushed against. 'Time to leave, *ma douce*. Let us see if we can whet and satisfy a different hunger.'

CHAPTER NINE

THE DRIVE BACK through the winding roads of Provence to his secluded chateau seemed to take hours rather than just twenty short minutes.

Benjamin had never known his veins to fizz as wildly as they were doing right then or been so aware of the heat of his skin. Freya stared out of the window beside him, her stillness absolute. Only the erratic rise and fall of her chest showed it to be nothing but a façade.

He could not believe how stunning she looked that day. Freya's striking looks had turned into a beauty that had stolen his breath so many times he was surprised he had any oxygen left in his lungs.

She'd chosen to marry him in a simple white silk dress that floated to her ankles, with a lace bodice that sparkled under the sun's rays held up by delicate spaghetti straps. On her feet were flat white sandals that suited the bohemian effect of the dress, her dark hair loose and falling in waves over her shoulders.

The dress she had chosen had hardly been a tra-ditional wedding dress but it had been perfect for their wedding. It had proven her commitment in the vows she was making.

Benjamin had taken one look at her and wished he'd arranged for them to exchange those vows in his chateau garden under an archway adorned with flowers of all different scents and colours.

They had left the town hall as husband and wife and stood together at the top of the steps, the photographer's lens trained on them exactly as Benjamin had instructed.

The sun's rays had bounced over Freya's skin and he had stared into eyes that were wide with trepidation, and felt that same dazzling punch in the guts he'd experienced the first time he'd set eyes on her. Just like that, the kiss he'd planned for the media's delectation and Javier's continued humiliation had seemed all wrong.

This was their wedding. Whatever the circumstances behind their vows, this was a commitment they were making to each other.

He didn't want to think about his nemesis.

Instead, he had put an arm around her and drawn her to him so her cheek rested against his chest. She had trembled in his arms.

It had come to him then as he inhaled her scent with the photographer's lens flashing at them why he needed their first kiss as husband and wife to be away from prying eyes…his need to possess

Freya had become stronger than his thirst for revenge against Javier.

When he kissed her next, he had no intention of stopping.

'The first time we drove this road together in the dark you had a can of pepper spray aimed at my face,' he commented idly as his driver took them through his forest.

They were almost home.

She didn't move her head from the window. 'I wish I had used it.'

'Do you think it would have changed the outcome between us?'

She raised a shoulder in a light shrug. 'If I hadn't left the hotel with you, if I had taken my chances at the airfield, if I had made a successful escape over your wall…any of those things could have changed the outcome.'

He reached a hand out to smooth a lock of her hair behind an ear.

'Do you wish you *had* been able to change it? Do you wish it had been Javier you exchanged your vows with today?'

She stilled, whether at his touch or his question he did not know.

Her throat moved before she said quietly, 'I married you. It is pointless wishing for an alternative reality.'

A stab of something that felt a little like how he imagined jealousy would feel cut into his chest.

That hadn't been a denial.

Freya had never given any indication that she harboured genuine feelings for Javier but nor had she given any indication that she didn't.

She desired him; that had been proven beyond doubt, but that didn't mean she didn't desire Javier too.

Had she spent their wedding day wishing she had married the other man? Was she approaching their wedding night wishing it were Javier's bed she would be sharing instead of his?

He rubbed his finger over the rim of her ear. Freya had such pretty, delicate ears…he had never thought of ears as pretty before. He had never noticed *anyone's* ears before.

He noticed everything about Freya. There was not a part of her face he wasn't now familiar with in a way he had never been familiar with another.

He could hardly wait to discover the parts she kept hidden from view. That time was almost with them and if she was approaching it wishing it were with Javier then he would make damn sure to drive his rival from her mind.

Come the morning her first thought would be him and him alone.

Come the morning and she would never wish she were with Javier or think of him again.

* * *

'Drink?'

Freya nodded tightly. Her knees shook so hard they could hardly support her weight. She had been unable to speak since they had walked back into the chateau to a vibrant display of flowers and balloons in the main reception room.

She had no idea where the staff were though. The chateau, normally bustling with unobtrusive life, was silent enough to hear a pin drop.

The silence in Benjamin's bedroom was even more oppressive. She fought the urge to bolt like a frightened colt.

'Take a seat.' He strolled to a dark wood cabinet, gesturing to the cosy armchair in the corner of his bedroom.

She sat and pressed her knees together under the wedding dress she knew wouldn't be covering her for much longer.

As terrified as she was at that moment, there was none of the coldness in her veins fear normally brought about. Instead there was heat, electricity zinging over her skin, dread and desire colliding.

Benjamin's quarters had a similar layout to her own but, where hers were painted in light, muted colours that had a decidedly feminine feel, his was much darker with a rich, masculine hue.

His bed…

She had never known beds that large existed.

She had never known beds could be a work of art in their own right. Made of a dark wood she didn't know the name of, it was clearly a bespoke creation, and covered in a beautiful silk-looking slate-grey duvet that must be bespoke too to fit the bed.

Freya breathed in deeply, trying her hardest to keep the trembles threatening to overwhelm her under control, looking everywhere but at that bed.

'Your drink, Madame Guillem.'

She had to hold herself back from snatching the glass from his hand and downing it all in one.

It wasn't the first time she had been addressed by her new title since the service but it was the first time Benjamin had said it.

She was thankful she hadn't downed her drink when she took the first big sip and tasted its potency. Benjamin had made her a gin and tonic that was definitely more gin than tonic and the one sip was enough to steady her nerves, if only momentarily.

He'd moved away from her again to return to the cabinet, dimming the lights on the way. A moment later, low music filled the room and broke the heavy, stifling silence.

She had never heard the song before but the singer's soulful baritone calmed her that little bit more. It didn't make it any easier for her to breathe though and she took another sip of her drink, her nerves back on tenterhooks as she waited for Benjamin to make his move.

He held a crystal tumbler of what she assumed to be Scotch in his hand and was wafting it gently under his nose while he stared at her, a meditative gleam in his green eyes. His gaze not dropping from hers, he drained his drink in one swallow and placed the empty tumbler on the cabinet.

Then he strode to her with a hand held out.

He didn't speak. He didn't need to.

She stared at the steady hand, so much larger than her own, taking in the masculine elegance of his long fingers before slipping her hand into it and wordlessly allowing him to help her to her feet.

At some point since they'd returned to his chateau, Benjamin had removed his tuxedo jacket and bow tie and undone the top two buttons of his white shirt. Freya had never seen him wear white before, black being his colour of choice, which she had assumed was to match his heart.

The white contrasted against the dark olive hue of his skin and even more starkly against the shadows the collar of his shirt made against his throat.

Her gaze rose with a will of its own to rest on his face and the eyes that had become as dark as the forests that surrounded his home.

The hand still holding hers tightened and she swayed forward so their faces were close enough for the warmth of his breath to whisper against her lips and suddenly she was taken by that same burst of desperate longing that had overcome her two months before when she had first seen him standing in Javier's garden.

This was the man who had haunted her dreams for two long months, the man she had been unable to stop herself obsessing over, the last man in the world she would have chosen to marry simply because he was the one man in the world who evoked this sick, desperate longing inside her with nothing more than a look and made her heart feel as if it could burst through her ribcage and soar like a songbird to lodge itself in his chest.

Their faces still close enough together that one tiny jolt forward would join their lips together, Benjamin's hold on her hand loosened. His fingers trailed up her arm to her shoulder, burning shivers trailing in their wake.

She closed her eyes to the sensation firing through her, the beats of her heart so loud they drowned out the music playing.

His hand now drew up her neck to burrow into her hair, the other splayed across her lower back. Her lips tingled as his warm breath drew closer, filling her mouth with moisture as his lips finally claimed hers.

The first press of his mouth against hers set off something inside her, a rush of need so powerful that she fought frantically against it, clenching her hands into fists to cling onto the last of her sanity before the desire dragged her down to a place she feared—the greatest of all her fears—she could never come back up from.

Since agreeing to marry him she had imagined herself playing the role of sacrificial virgin, lying on the bed and letting him take what he wanted but giving nothing back. She had known that to remain passive would take the greatest self-control of her life, especially after the kiss they had shared, but it was only as his tongue danced into her mouth that she understood how futile a hope it had been. Her hunger for him…it was too much. With a sigh that could have been a moan, she swayed into the strength of his solid body and welcomed the heat of his hungry kisses.

Her movement set something off in him too. The hands securing her gently tightened and then she was on her toes, crushed against him, breasts against chest, pelvis against abdomen, her hands winding around his neck, her fingers digging into the nape of his neck, her tongue dancing against his. And it was his hands now sweeping over her back and up her sides, brushing the underside of her breasts, the ferocity of their kisses intensifying with every passing second. Every time he touched her bare skin she felt the mark of his skin against hers and her hunger grew.

She was so caught up in their kisses she only

realised he'd pulled the zip of her dress down her back when his hand slid into the opened space and dipped down to clasp her bottom.

Her breaths shallow, she moved her face to stare at him, terror making its return.

She had to tell him, she thought wildly. If she didn't…

'Benjamin…'

But he'd taken the skinny straps of her dress and skimmed them down her arms. She had hardly spoken the last syllable of his name before gravity pulled her dress down, her lean body offering it no resistance so it fell into a pool at her feet leaving her naked bar her plain, cotton knickers.

Her arms flailed to cover her breasts, panic now clawing at her.

Nudity was no big deal to her, it couldn't be. She danced without wearing underwear, as most dancers did. She had never been body-conscious, never been one to torment herself over her shape. She ate the best diet she could and worked hard to keep her body lean and supple so she had every tool she could to be the best dancer she could be.

But she had never been virtually naked in front of a man who wasn't looking at her as a dancer but as a lover.

She hadn't had an hour of meditation and yoga to calm her mind as she had when he'd walked into her quarters the other day.

Never, until that moment, had she felt truly naked.

Her breasts were *tiny*, she thought hopelessly. She didn't have the curves other women had.

Benjamin had stepped back to look at her, and she cringed to see the frown on his face.

Then the frown softened and his hands rested on her arms that still desperately covered her breasts. Gripping them lightly, he slowly pulled them apart to expose her for his scrutiny.

Her mortification grew when he let go of her arms so they hung by her hips, her fingers twitching to cover her breasts again.

He stepped back again then slowly walked around her. She could feel the stare of his eyes penetrating her skin and could do nothing to stop the trembling of her legs.

She was exposing herself in a way she had spent years fighting to keep covered, not her external flesh but what lay beneath it, the sensuality that lay beneath her skin, the only part of herself that was hers alone, never to be given, never to be shared, the only part of herself she'd been able to keep *for* herself.

It was slipping through her fingers and the harder she tried to keep control of it, the more it pulled away from her and into Benjamin's hands...

When he finally stood in front of her again he placed a finger on her lips and leaned in to nuzzle his lips against her ear. *'Tu es belle, ma douce.'*

She was stunned at the tenderness in his voice even if she didn't understand the words, her breath leaving her again as he moved his finger from her lips to cover her cheeks with the whole of his hands and stare hard into her eyes.

'You are beautiful, Freya.'

His lips brushed against hers before brushing over her jaw to burrow into her neck. Then he sank onto his knees so his face was level with her breasts.

He stared at them before covering them entirely with his hands. He gazed up at her. 'They are perfect. *You* are perfect.'

She couldn't breathe. Her throat had closed, fresh sensation bubbling inside her, the hunger in his eyes driving out the panic.

Then he slid his hands sensuously over her stomach to grip her hips and covered her breasts with his mouth.

At the first flick of his tongue over her nipple she gasped, her hands flailing to rest on his shoulders.

Sensation suffused her, intensifying as he took one breast into his mouth, his obvious delight in them and the thrills shooting through her veins driving the last of her embarrassment and fear clean out of her.

Benjamin felt Freya's sharp nails dig through his shirt and into his skin, the most pleasurable pain of his life.

For two months he had dreamed of this moment; dreamed of Freya coming undone in his arms, imagined her naked and fantasised about all the things he wanted to do with her.

This was beyond anything his feeble imagination could have dreamt up, and they had barely begun.

Her breasts were the smallest he had ever seen but they were the most beautiful. He hadn't been lying when he had called them perfect. Perfectly round, perfectly high and the perfect fit for his mouth.

They had the perfect taste too.

She had the perfect taste.

Slowly he trailed his mouth down her stomach, revelling in the smooth perfection of her skin, thrilling at the quiver of her belly when he licked it and the ragged movement of her chest as she struggled to breathe, knowing it was her response to *him* causing it.

His own breaths had become ragged too. The tightness in his groin was almost intolerable, his need for relief a burn that he willingly ignored, too intent on seducing this beautiful woman—his *wife*—to care for his own needs.

His time would come.

Lower down he went, raining soft kisses over her abdomen to the band of her underwear, the heat inside him rising as he got closer to her womanly heat.

Pinching the elastic of her knickers in his fingers, he gently tugged them down her hips to her supple yet shaking thighs.

He touched his nose to the soft hair between her legs and breathed deeply.

About to nuzzle lower, he became dimly aware that her fingers, which had been digging into his scalp, had stopped moving.

Looking up, he found her staring down at him with what could only be described as terror in her eyes.

It stopped him in his tracks.

'Have you not done this before?' he asked slowly.

She hesitated before giving a jerky shake of her head.

His brain racing, he pressed a tender kiss into the downy hair, inhaled her intoxicating scent one more time and tugged the underwear back up to cover her.

Freya had less experience than he had thought...

Getting back to his feet, he pressed himself close to her quivering body and gently kissed her, then lifted her into his arms.

There was no resistance. She wound her arms around his neck and gazed into his eyes as he carried her to the bed.

Laying her down, he kissed her again, more deeply, before dipping his face into the elegant arch of her neck and tenderly nipping the skin with his teeth.

'I have too many clothes on,' he said into her neck, then pressed a kiss against the pulse beating wildly at the base of her jawline and sat up.

The obsidian of her eyes seemed to glow with the weight of a thousand emotions. She raised a hand as if to reach out and touch him then swallowed. The hand fell back to her side.

He picked it up and razed a kiss across the knuckles. *'Tu es belle.'*

She *was* beautiful. Mesmerising.

Her lips quirked in the glimmer of a smile and her chest rose as she took a deep breath.

Not taking his gaze from her face, Benjamin proceeded to undress, first his shirt, then getting to his feet to tug his trousers and underwear off until he was fully naked. He'd been so caught up in his seduction of Freya and the headiness of the moment that he hadn't appreciated how constricting his clothes had been until he took them off and his arousal sprang free.

Resisting the urge to take it in his hand, he sat back on the bed. 'Now you are the one with too many clothes on,' he said with a lightness that belied the heavy thuds of his heart, tracing his finger in a line from the dip at the top of her neck, down between her breasts and over the flat plain of her stomach to rest on the band of her knickers.

Dieu, he could devour her whole.

Her hands clenched into fists, her breaths becoming ragged again. He took hold of both her wrists and slowly spread them up to rest either side of her head as he laid himself over her until he covered her, propping his weight up on his elbows to gaze into her pulsating eyes.

Then he kissed her.

As their mouths moved together, fused into one, the passion reigniting and deepening, he loosened his hold on her wrists and laced his fingers through hers. She squeezed in response then dragged them away to wrap her arms around his neck and pull him down so his weight was fully on her.

He groaned at the sensation of her breasts pressed so tightly against his chest and kissed her more deeply. His skin was alive with heat that seeped through his veins and deep into his bones, all thoughts leaving him except one; the one that needed to touch and taste every part of this beautiful woman who had been in his head for so long and now lay in his bed and in his blood.

With his mouth and hands he began his exploration, discovering the parts of her body that made her suck in a breath at his touch, the parts that made her moan, the parts that made her nails dig into his flesh, feeling her relax so much that when he pressed his mouth to her pelvis again, she sighed and her left leg writhed.

Encouraged, Benjamin slowly tugged her knickers down, making a trail with his tongue down her legs in its wake before kissing his way back up and inhaling the scent of her heat without any barrier at all.

She stilled.

For a long time he didn't move, waiting to see what she would do.

Then he felt the whisper of her hand on his head, her fingers threading through his hair…

He traced his tongue between the damp folds and heard her gasp. Her fingers made twisting motions in his hair that pulled when he found her secret nub and her bottom lifted.

Dieu.

With all the languid care in the world, he made love to her with his mouth, relishing the taste of her sweet muskiness on his tongue, letting her responses, which were becoming more overt by the second, guide him as to what was giving her the greatest pleasure, intent only *on* her pleasure, Freya's pleasure, Freya, this beautiful, beautiful woman he ached to make completely his.

Only when he was sure that she was nearing her peak and completely ready for him did he slide his tongue back up her stomach, nipping each of her breasts with his teeth as he went, to reclaim her mouth and gently part her thighs.

Guiding his erection to the warmth of her heat he closed his eyes and gritted his teeth.

This was a moment to savour.

Inhaling deeply through his nose, he covered her mouth with his then could hold on no longer. With one long thrust, he buried himself deep inside her…

Freya felt a momentary sharpness that she would probably have missed if she hadn't been waiting for it, then there was nothing but sensation, every single nerve ending inside her sighing and delighting in the feel of Benjamin finally inside her, filling her completely.

She gazed into the green eyes that were staring at her with such hunger, and touched his face before lifting her head to kiss him.

How she loved his kisses. Loved his tongue taking such rough possession of hers. Loved his touch. Loved the feel of his broad chest covering hers, the dark hairs brushing against her breasts. Loved what he was doing to her right then…

Ohhhhh…

Her head fell back on the pillow as he began to move. He withdrew slowly only to plunge into her again. And then he did it again, and again, over and over, somehow knowing exactly what she wanted and what she needed, all the things about herself she hadn't known.

The last of the fight had left her when he'd carried her to the bed and laid her down so tenderly, almost as if she were precious to him…

And then he had kissed and stroked all her defences and fears away until sanity had ceased to matter. Nothing mattered. Nothing apart from *this*; here, now, them, together.

She'd had no idea that she could feel such things. And the sensations ravaging her were heightening.

As Benjamin's movements grew wilder, his breath hot on her face, his groans soaking into her skin, the throbbing ache deep within her tightened and burned into a flame. Hotter and hotter it grew, blazing into a peak that came to a crescendo...

And then she was soaring, sparks exploding through her on a riptide of pleasure she had never, never, imagined possible.

Hazily she was aware that Benjamin had let go too, burying his face in her hair with a ragged, drawn-out moan.

She held him tightly as they rocked together, holding on to the pleasure for as long as they could until, finally, they both stilled and all that was left of the explosion were tiny glowing flickers that tingled and buzzed through and over every part of her.

CHAPTER TEN

FREYA LOST ALL semblance of time as she lay there with Benjamin's weight so deliciously compressing on her. They could have lain there for minutes or hours.

She opened her eyes. She felt so profoundly different from when she had walked into this room that she half expected the room to look different too.

The dim lights were still on. The music Benjamin had put on still played, a different song now worming its way through her slowly de-fuzzing head.

'Okay?' His question came as a murmur yet cut through the silence as if he had shouted it.

Her throat closed and she had to breathe deeply to get air into her suddenly constricted lungs.

'Fine,' she managed.

He rolled off her and onto his back, though kept his head turned so he faced her. 'You are sure?'

She wanted to offer a pithy comment, something that would negate the huge whirl of emotions filling her, to deny the wondrousness of what she had just experienced and which she knew, as pathetically inexperienced as she had been, that he had shared too.

But she couldn't. Somehow this man who was still very much a stranger even if he was her husband… He had made her feel beautiful. He had recognised her fear and inexperience and made love to her as if she were someone to cherish.

She would not let fear demean or diminish it.

Slowly she turned her head to look into the eyes that always saw too much, and nodded.

He studied her for long moments before craning his neck to kiss her gently. 'I'm going to turn the music off. Can I get you a drink?'

'No, thank you.'

He kissed her again then turned over and climbed off the bed.

She watched him stride to the sound system, completely at ease in his skin.

And no wonder. Until that moment she hadn't looked at him properly. She'd gazed at his broad chest and felt it crushed against her, seen his strong, muscular arms and felt them bunch in her hands, the rest of him only glimpsed at, even the long legs she'd wound her own around.

She'd thought of him as having the stalking grace of a panther but only now, seeing him unashamedly naked, all the components that made him Benjamin put together, did she fully appreciate his rugged masculine beauty. It made the breath catch in her throat…

'You like what you see?'

She blinked, suddenly aware she had been staring at him.

Cheeks flaming, she then became aware that she had been staring at him naked, forgetting her own nakedness.

The hazy glow of their lovemaking had gone and with it her confidence to be naked around this man.

He'd cast her in a spell. He must have done.

She had done more than bare herself to him, she had given the essence of herself. She had lost control.

He'd made her forget. Forget what he'd done. Forget who she was and all the reasons she needed to keep an emotional distance from him.

His lovemaking had been incredible…*they* had been incredible. Just as she had feared.

'I like what *I* see,' he murmured, seemingly unfazed by her silence.

She averted her eyes from his gleaming scrutiny and, keeping her thighs together to protect her modesty as best she could, grabbed the duvet, which their lovemaking had dislodged and managed to heap into a pile, and burrowed low into it.

He laughed lightly. 'I have embarrassed you.'

She sensed him treading back to his side of the

bed and wished she could escape to the solitude of her own quarters.

A breeze fluttered against her back, Benjamin lifting the duvet to climb back in beside her. As she waited for the bed to dip, holding the part of the duvet she was wrapped in tightly, she became aware of a silence.

Coldness crept up her spine that had nothing to do with her back being exposed as the silence drew out and she was on the verge of saying something to break it when he finally got into bed.

She held her breath, squeezed her eyes shut and waited for him to turn off the dim lights. If she kept her back to him and played dead he might leave her alone.

Don't touch me, she silently begged. *Your touch is too much. Please, don't make me lose any more of myself than I already have.*

But the question he posed into the silence made her wish he had touched her instead.

'You were a *virgin*?'

What else explained the small, red stain marking the under-sheet of his bed? Benjamin wondered, his mind reeling. He'd seen it as he'd pulled the duvet back and his blood had run from languidly sated to ice cold in an instant.

Freya had been more than merely inexperienced. She'd been a virgin.

His chest tightened.

Why hadn't she told him?

Slowly she rolled over, her black orbs fixing straight onto him.

The tightness in his chest turned into a cramp.

For a long time neither of them spoke.

'You were a virgin.' This time he posed it as a statement.

She gave the briefest, jerkiest of nods.

'Why didn't you tell me?'

She swallowed and blinked rapidly. 'I couldn't.'

'Why not?'

Clenching her jaw, she shrugged.

'If I'd had the slightest idea you were a virgin, I would never...'

'Never have *what*?' she interrupted, suddenly fierce, her neck and face turning the colour of crimson, the obsidian in her eyes spitting at him. 'Stolen me? Blackmailed me? Wrecked my life? Forced me to give up my job in a company I love? Does my being a virgin somehow *improve* me? Does my innocence make me a better, more worthy person?'

The tenderness he'd felt towards her vanished as a flash of lava-like anger coursed through him. At her. At himself.

At himself for blackmailing a virgin into marriage.

At Freya for putting money above her own morals, or whatever it was that had caused her to reach the age of twenty-three years untouched.

'Innocent? You signed a contract exchanging your body for money!'

'No, I signed a contract of *marriage*. You read that contract without any context and made assumptions about me because it suited your agenda. Not once did you ask *why* I chose to sign it. You were determined to punish Javier and to hell with who got hurt while you did it.'

'You wanted the money. You made that very clear.' He leaned forward so his nose almost touched hers, delivering his words with ice-cold precision. 'Paint yourself as a sainted martyr if you must but no one forced you to sign those contracts. No one forced you to marry me. No one forced you into my bed, and no one, *no one*, forced you to enjoy being in it.'

Her face became aflame with colour but she didn't back down. 'Who said I enjoyed it?'

He slid his hand around her neck and rested his cheek against hers, ignoring her attempt to rear out of his hold. Speaking into her ear, he whispered, 'You came undone in my arms, *ma douce*, and that is why you are so angry now. You hate that you desire me and you hate that what we just shared proves the self-control you take such pride in is built on sand. If I were to kiss you now, you would come undone all over again.'

'Get your hands off me,' she said with such venom her words landed like barbs on his skin.

'Do not forget my body belongs to me. I am not your chattel.'

He did more than move away from her, he threw the duvet off and climbed out of the bed to stride to his bathroom. Over his shoulder, as if delivering a throwaway comment, he said, 'I'm going to take a shower. Feel free to use my absence to return to your own quarters.'

He could feel the burn of her stare as he locked the bathroom door.

Alone, he pressed the palms of his hands tightly against the cool white tiles and took a deep breath, then another, and another, fighting the urge to punch the walls until his knuckles bled.

The world had turned itself upside down in a matter of seconds.

Dieu, she had been a virgin.

Stepping into the shower, he turned the temperature up as high as he could bear and scrubbed vigorously at his skin, determined to rid himself of the grubby, scaly feeling cloying in his pores.

When he'd finally rubbed himself raw and returned to the bedroom, Freya had gone.

'This is where you've been hiding.'

Freya looked up from the bench she was sitting on under the cherry tree, shielding her eyes from the sun with her hand.

Benjamin walked towards her, a bottle of water in his hand, a wary smile on his face.

'I've been looking for you,' he explained with a shrug.

Feigning nonchalance at his unexpected appearance although her heart immediately set off at a canter, she stretched her legs out. On this scorching summer's day, he'd dressed in black jeans and a dark blue shirt, his only concession to the sun his rolled-up sleeves. She couldn't detect an ounce of perspiration on him whereas little beads trickled down her spine even though she wore a cotton summer dress.

'I went for a walk.' She fixed her gaze on the spectacular view surrounding her.

She had woken before the sun, everything that had passed between them that night flashing through her on a reel before she'd been fully conscious, sending her jumping out of the bed and into the shower.

So early had it been that when she'd hurried to the kitchen not a single member of staff had been awake.

She'd found an avocado and a banana that would suffice for her breakfast and forced them down her cramped throat and stomach. And then she had set off, walking the forests and fields of his estate, keeping her legs moving, *needing* to keep them moving, her usual way of expelling her emotions still denied her and would always be denied when she resided under Benjamin's roof.

She had never needed to dance as much as she did then, never felt that the fabric of her being could fray at the seams without the glue she had learned to depend on.

He sat next to her and offered her the water bottle.

'Thank you.' She took it from his hand being careful not to let their fingers brush, instinctively knowing just one touch would be her undoing.

She needed to keep her focus. Had to. She would not let what was happening inside her derail the future she had worked so hard for and which her parents had sacrificed so much for.

But Benjamin awoke her senses so they all tuned into his frequency just with his presence. Her nose begged her to lean closer so she could smell his gorgeous scent better, her fingers itched to slide over and touch those muscular thighs inches from her own...

She didn't want this. Not any of it. When he'd asked after the wedding if she wished she'd married Javier instead, the answer that had screamed through her head had been a resounding *yes*.

And that had been before they had made love.

If she'd married Javier there wouldn't have been any of this angst tormenting her, there would have been only indifference. None of the hate. None of the passion.

None of the joy she had discovered in Benjamin's arms...

Hands trembling, she drank heavily from the water bottle then wiped the rim and handed it back.

Silence fell between them until he broke it by saying, 'This was my mother's favourite spot.'

Freya had discovered this unexpected patch of paradise by accident a few days ago. The bench and its overhanging cherry tree were in a small clearing accessed through a short cut-through in his forest, sitting on the crest of a hill. Fields of all colours sprawled out for miles below them.

It was just a bench under a cherry tree but there was something so calming about the setting she'd sought it out again.

'Was this your family home?' she asked.

'My family home was in a suburb of Paris. My mother always said she would move to Provence when her children were grown up and Clara retired from the ballet.'

'Clara Casillas?'

He nodded. 'My mother was her seamstress. She worked for the ballet company in Paris where Clara first made her name. Remember I told you of the closeness between them? Clara refused to let anyone else make her costumes. They denied it but I am sure they deliberately got pregnant at the same time so they could raise their babies together.'

'You and the Casillas brothers?' she asked cautiously, afraid to break their tenuous cordiality by saying the names she knew were like a red rag to a bull.

Another nod. 'We saw the world with them.'

'You were lucky. I would have loved to have seen her perform in the flesh.'

'I found the ballet as boring as hell. I wanted to play football, not be stuck in a theatre. But I had Javier and Luis. We would sneak off together and kick drink cans in theatre car parks or try and spy on the dancers undressing. We had the run of the backstage when performances were on and we made the most of it.'

A bubble of laughter burst from her lungs. 'I can't imagine Javier doing any of that.'

He met her eye, a tinge of amusement in his stare. 'He joined in grudgingly—he was always the serious one. Luis and I were always the instigators of any trouble.'

'Did Chloe not join in?'

'We were ten when she was born. By the time she was old enough to get into trouble with us it was over.'

Neither of them needed to say why it had been over. The story of Clara Casillas's death at the hands of her own husband was still a tale rehashed *ad nauseam* by the press and ghoulish television producers. The friendship between Benjamin and the Casillas brothers had endured…until mere weeks ago.

'Did your mother buy the chateau after Clara died?' she asked.

'She was a single mother by then—my parents divorced when she fell pregnant with Chloe. I bought the chateau for her to end her days in when we learned the treatment for her cancer had failed. I would carry her here to sit on this bench when she was too weak to walk any more.' He lifted his head to look up at the branches of the cherry tree hanging sweetly over them. 'We planted this tree when she died seven years ago. Her ashes are buried under it.'

Freya jumped up. 'I'm sorry. I had no idea…'

'Sit back down, *ma douce*. This is not a shrine for her. It is a celebration of her memory, and if there is an afterlife I know my mother will be delighted that you, a dancer she would have loved, were sitting in the spot she loved so much and enjoying the same views that gave her such peace. Please, sit.'

She sat back down gingerly, trying to process what he'd just revealed to her.

Benjamin had said his mother died seven years ago. Hadn't he said before that Javier and Luis had gone to him for the money they'd needed to buy the land for the Tour Mont Blanc building seven years ago too?

These were both things she already knew but only now did she put the two dates together.

Had they gone to him when his mother was dying? Had they taken advantage of the grief he must have been dealing with—and she knew what that felt like, a ticking time-bomb hanging over your head…?

'Javier and Luis were with me when we planted the tree,' he said, breaking into her thoughts with words that made her certain he'd been able to read what she'd been thinking. 'She loved them. I thought they loved her too. The night Clara was killed, it was my mother who comforted them…'

'You were there that night?' That was not something she had known.

He nodded. His jaw had tightened. 'It was after the performance. We were in a hotel across the road from the theatre babysitting Chloe so none of us were there to see or hear what went on between them. My mother woke us to tell the news. She held those boys in her arms the whole night. After they were taken to Spain by their grandparents, my mother made sure they still saw us. They stayed with us many times.' Benjamin swallowed the bile forming in his throat. 'After Clara died, Javier and Luis's visits were the only things that could make her smile. She became like their second mother. They visited her when she was ill. Luis visited so many times the hospital staff assumed he was her son. She never corrected them. She liked them thinking that.'

He had no idea why he was revealing all this to her. These were things he never spoke of.

But the past had become so entwined with the present in recent months that he found it a relief to finally speak of it.

In truth, he owed it to her. Freya deserved to know.

What had she said that first night, about being able to sleep soundly? That his conscience should prevent it?

He understood now what she'd meant. His sleep had been fractured, in and out of wakefulness, his mind a constant whirl.

He still couldn't believe she had been a virgin, did not see how it was possible to reach the age of twenty-three untouched, especially in the hotbed of the ballet world. But the proof had been there, undeniable.

He'd taken her virginity and the more it played on his mind, the worse he felt, sicker in himself.

Her husky voice carried through the humid air. 'When did they ask you for the money?'

'The day she got the terminal diagnosis. They knew I had the money.' He looked at her, his heart tugging to see the glimmer of compassion ringing in eyes that normally only rang with loathing. 'I knew my mother wasn't going to survive it even before we had it confirmed. I'd already made up my mind to buy the chateau for her.'

He'd known the romance of its architecture and its spectacular views would be a tonic to his mother's cancer-ravaged body and he'd been right. She had spent the last three months of her life there and slipped away peacefully.

He had kept the dire financial situation buying the chateau had left him in from her.

He cleared his throat before continuing. 'I had the cash available to buy it outright. It was a lot of money. The chateau had undergone a complete renovation so was priced high.'

'They knew?'

'Of course they knew.' He didn't hide his bitterness. 'They knew everything. They knew taking my money to finance Tour Mont Blanc meant I would have to take a mortgage to buy the chateau. They knew I overextended myself. They knew when I got into financial trouble over it and was on the verge of bankruptcy. They knew I only gave them that investment because it was them and I trusted them as if they were my own blood. I never blamed them for the situation I got myself in but I gave them that money in good faith and then I learned they had taken it in bad. They knew the terms we agreed verbally were different from the terms on the contract.'

'So your revenge really wasn't about the money then,' she said in the softest tone he had ever heard from her lips. 'They hurt you.'

'They did not hurt me,' he dismissed. 'They betrayed me and kept the lie going for seven years. I was going to donate the profit to a charity that helps traumatised kids. Javier and Luis had to deal with one of the most traumatic things a child could go through but they had been lucky to have family and my mother to help pick up the pieces. Other children aren't so lucky or resilient. They haven't just stolen from me but those children too. I'm fortunate that all the hard work I've put into the business in the past seven years has left me with a sizeable fortune. I'm in the process of liquidating some assets so I can still donate the money but it should never have come to this. They are thieves. They have stolen my money and robbed me of my childhood memories. Everything is tainted now. I think of them carrying my mother's coffin with me into the church and want to rip their heads from their necks.'

He closed his eyes and took a deep breath. Beside him, Freya remained silent but he could feel something new emanating from her that he had never felt before, something that was neither loathing nor desire and flowed into his skin like a balm.

'Do you feel better now you have taken me from Javier?' There was no malice in her voice, just simple, gentle curiosity. 'Do you feel avenged?'

'There is some satisfaction to be had but do I feel avenged…? When I have had my revenge on Luis too, *then* I will feel avenged.'

'What are you planning to do to him?'

'I am still thinking.' *Trying* to think. His thought process had been awry since Freya had been under his roof, her presence even when not in the same room taking all his focus.

'I don't suppose there's any point in saying that sometimes it is better for the soul to let things go,' she said quietly. 'But I will say this—please, for the sake of your soul, don't involve anyone else in it. This is between you and the Casillas brothers. Don't let anyone else suffer for it.'

'I don't want you to suffer.' He took another deep breath and looked up at the cobalt sky, the distant wispy trail of an aeroplane the only thing to cut through the skyscape, then got to his feet. 'Come back to the chateau with me. I have something to show you which, I hope, will make you feel more at home here.'

'What is it?'

'The reason I spent an hour searching for you. Your wedding present from me.'

CHAPTER ELEVEN

FREYA FOLLOWED BENJAMIN into the chateau and up the stairs, apprehension colliding with the ache in her heart at all he had confided in her and which she needed to sit down and think about properly to digest.

She had never thought her heart would ache for him but it did. Badly.

How could Javier treat his oldest friend in that way? And she didn't doubt a word of it. What he and Luis had done was so much worse than merely ripping him off of a fortune. It was a betrayal of biblical proportions.

She shivered to think that was the behaviour of the man she had intended to marry.

When they reached the second floor, Benjamin stopped outside a door that was, she judged, positioned above his own quarters. This was a floor of the chateau she had made a cursory search of on her first day when seeking a dance space and quickly forgotten about. All the rooms up there were laid in thick carpet that would act like a grip on her pointe shoes.

His eyes were on her. 'Open it.'

'It's not a cell, is it?' she asked with a nervous laugh.

He shook his head. 'For once trust me and open the door.'

She stifled the instinctive retort of trust having to be earned.

Benjamin had opened himself up to her. Only a small part, she knew, but it was enough for her to see him with eyes not quite so prejudiced.

He'd made an effort to build a bridge between them and for that she would, this once, place her trust in him and do as he asked.

Holding her breath, Freya opened the door a crack and peered through. The smell of fresh paint hit her immediately.

Then she blinked, certain she was seeing things. But no, she wasn't seeing things. This was a dance studio.

She pushed the door fully open and stared in stunned, disbelieving awe at what had been revealed before her.

Benjamin folded his arms over his chest as he waited for Freya's response. Since opening the door and stepping into the newly revealed room, she hadn't moved a muscle. He didn't think she'd even taken a breath.

'What do you think?' he asked roughly. His heart

beat heavily through the tightness in his chest, his stomach twisting.

She shook her head, her throat moving, then slowly turned her head to look at him. Her black eyes were wide and shining. 'You did this...for *me*?'

'You're a professional dancer. You need to practise.'

She needed to dance. Freya was a woman with ballet flowing in her veins, ballet the air she breathed. To deny her the opportunity to dance in the chateau was tantamount to torture.

She raised a hand that had a slight tremor in it to her mouth. 'I don't know what to say.'

'You can say whether you like it or not,' he commented wryly.

She blinked and gave a muffled laugh. 'I can't believe this.'

'Is it suitable for your needs?'

'It's perfect. Beautiful. Just beautiful. And it's so light and high.' She drifted forward into the centre of the huge room, her head now turning in all directions, then stopped when she caught his reflection in the walled mirror. Her forehead creased. 'How did you do it? *When* did you do it?'

'This week. When we agreed to marry.'

'But how?'

'By calling the director of a Parisian ballet company for guidance and employing a top building team.'

'But *how*?' she repeated.

'By paying them ten times their usual rate to stop what they were doing to make it happen. I had hoped it would be completed for our wedding so I could surprise you with it then but there was a delay with the flooring.' Specialist flooring for dancers.

'How?' she virtually shrieked, bouncing on her toes and waving her arms in the air. 'From conception to finished product in…what? Five days? How is that even possible? How many rooms were knocked down?'

'Only three.'

'Only? You knocked three rooms into…*this*, and I didn't have a clue. I didn't hear anything or see anything, not even a single contractor.'

'They used the tradesman's entrance. The walls were knocked down when you were on your walks.'

'But…'

'No more questions about it. It is done and it is for you. I appreciate you will not spend many nights here once your break is over but this is your home now and when you are here I want you to feel at home.'

The animation that had overtaken her limbs disappeared as she stilled. An emotion he didn't recognise flickered over her face. She chewed at her lip as she stared at him, the intensity of her gaze seeming to cut through the distance between them and burn straight in his chest...

Backing away from her with lungs so tight he could hardly pull air into them, he said, 'I have work to get on with so I shall leave you to enjoy your new dance studio. If there is anything you are not happy with, tell me and we shall change it.'

He left the studio in quick strides and had reached the top of the stairs when she called after him. 'Benjamin?'

It was the first time she'd called him by his name.

'*Oui?*'

'Thank you.'

'*De rien.* Enjoy your dancing. I will see you at dinner.'

Freya sat in the middle of the wonderful dance studio Benjamin had created, just for her, soaking it all in with a heart thumping so madly she was surprised her ribs didn't crack with the force.

This was a studio every little girl who dreamed of being a ballerina dreamed of dancing in. The left wall was a mirror, the rest painted soft white, a barre traversing the entire room, broken only by a huge round window at the far end, a floor-to-ceiling cupboard by the door and a beautiful high table next to it.

Eventually she pulled herself out of her stupor, got to her feet and opened the cupboard.

Inside it lay rows of pointe shoes, rows of ballet slippers all lying below a row of assorted practice outfits. They were all her exact size.

Further exploration revealed the tools needed to soften the pointe shoes and she pounced on them with glee.

Ignoring the cosy armchair placed in the corner, she sat cross-legged on the floor and began to massage the stiff toe cup, then, when she felt it was softened sufficiently, moved on to the shank, the hard sole that supported the arch of her foot, and gently bent it back and forth at the three-quarter mark. When she was happy with both shoes— by now convinced Benjamin had got Compania de Ballet de Casillas own shoemakers to provide them for her, the shoes' response to her well-practised manipulations rendering the alcohol spray and hammer often used to soften them redundant—she stripped her clothes off, pulled on a pair of tights and a leotard, and put the softened pointe shoes on, binding the ribbons securely.

Atop the table next to the cupboard sat a small sound system. Preloaded into it was the music for every ballet that had ever been created.

She found the music to Prokofiev's *Romeo and Juliet*, still her favourite after all these years, and pressed play.

Music filled the room, startling her into spinning round and gazing up at the ceiling where she spotted small, unobtrusive speakers placed at strategic intervals.

She covered her mouth as fresh emotion filled her.

Benjamin had done this, all of this, for her.

She blinked to focus herself and stood by the barre to begin simple stretching exercises that would warm her body and limber her up. A dancer's life was fraught with injury and not doing enough of a warm-up beforehand was a shortcut to a sprain or strain, as was a hard floor that didn't have any buoyancy for the inevitable falls.

Benjamin had had a semi-sprung sub-floor fitted that would be the perfect cushion for her falls.

The exercises she did were moves she had made thousands of times and the familiarity of them and the comfort of the music settled her stomach into an ease she had begun to fear she would never find again.

Her mind began to drift as it always did when doing her barre exercises alone. She imagined herself dancing the balcony scene where Romeo and Juliet danced the *pas de deux*, imagining it as she always did when visualising this scene, with a faceless partner.

But this time the imaginary faceless partner didn't remain faceless for long.

It was Benjamin's face that flowed through her mind, his strong arms around her waist then lift-

ing her into the air, his green eyes burning with
longing into hers…

An ache ripped through her, pulling the air from
her lungs with its force, the strength so powerful
that she dragged herself from her trance-like state
to rush to the sound system and skip to the Dance
of the Knights, breathing heavily, fear gripping her.

A knock on the door should have been a welcome distraction but what if it was him, catching
her now, at this moment when she couldn't trust
herself not to fly into his arms and beg him to make
love to her again?

Benjamin had *stolen* her, she reminded herself,
again, desperately.

She had insisted on this marriage because there
had been no other choice.

But Benjamin had knocked down three rooms in
his chateau to create a dance studio any ballerina
would want to die in, and he had done that for her.
He'd been under no obligation. He got nothing out
of it for himself.

This was the man who had almost bankrupted
himself so his mother could live the last of her life
in beauty.

Her heart heavy though a little calmer, she
braced herself before opening the door.

Christabel stood there with a tray and a smile.
'Monsieur Guillem thought you would be hungry.
Chef has made you a whole grain tortilla wrap with

avocado, chicken, tomato and lettuce. She can make you something else if…'

'This is perfect,' Freya interrupted with a grateful smile. Benjamin's chef had proven herself to be a shining star, keen to provide the resident ballerina with the nutritious meals she depended on and make them as appetising as they could be. Freya had never eaten so well and had not been in the least surprised to learn the chef had once been awarded her own Michelin star.

Once Christabel had gone, Freya poured herself a glass of iced water from the jug delivered with her wrap and ignored the armchair to sit on the curved ledge of the enormous round window.

Chewing slowly, she gazed out. The window overlooked the back garden giving her the perfect view to appreciate the stunning landscape, including the cherubic fountain in the centre that wouldn't have looked out of place in the palace of Versailles.

Slowly but surely she was starting to appreciate the beauty of Benjamin's chateau without angry eyes, like a filter being removed from the lens to reveal it in all its glory.

This was a chateau childish dreams were made of.

And now, with this wonderful studio, she had a place in it that was all her own.

Maybe one day it really would feel like home to her.

When she was about to pop the last bite of her delicious wrap into her mouth, her heart leapt into it instead as she saw Benjamin stroll by talking animatedly on his phone.

Her leaping heart began to beat so hard it became a heavy thrum and she found herself unable to tear her eyes away. Her suddenly greedy eyes soaked in everything about him, from the way his long, muscular legs filled the black jeans he wore and the way his muscles bunched beneath his black T-shirt…he had changed his clothing since he had left her in the studio. Even with her distance she could see how untamed his thick black hair had become and the shadow on his jaw hinting at black stubble about to break free… She had never seen a more rampantly masculine sight and it filled her with a longing that kept her rooted, right until the moment he turned his head.

She pressed her back into the curve of the window quickly before he could look up and see her staring down at him.

'You are happy with your studio?' Benjamin asked that evening as they dined together. This evening he had decided to eat the same meal as Freya, pork tenderloin with a lentil salad that he found, to his utmost surprise, to be extremely tasty. It wasn't quite hitting the spot the way his rich meals usually did but that would be rectified by the cheeses he liked to finish his meals with.

She lifted her eyes from her plate to his and gave a dreamy sigh. 'It's…perfect. I'm still rather over-awed, to be honest.'

'As long as you are happy with it that is all that matters.' He reached for his glass of white wine. Freya, as usual, had stuck to water, the wine glass laid out for her as usual remaining empty.

'I am.' She looked, if not happy, then more con-tent than he had ever seen her. Her time spent in her new studio seemed to have freed something inside her, all her hostility towards him gone.

'*Bien.* I hope you are as happy with the houses my employee has found for you. I've had him searching for an apartment in Madrid…' he found himself almost choking at the word '…and a house in London as per the terms of our contract. He has narrowed them down to a choice of five for each. I will forward the email with all the details to you later.'

'Thank you.'

'I assume you will want to view your preferred ones?'

'Just the London ones. The Madrid apartment is only going to be somewhere for me to sleep so don't bother with anything fancy as it will be a waste.'

The relief at this was dimmed by what it represented. If she only intended to use the Madrid apartment as a base to rest her head, what did that mean for the London house?

'I have appointments in Greece on Friday but we can fly over on Saturday. Tell me which ones you like the look of and I will get Giles to book viewings.'

He waited for her to respond, his sharp eyes noting she was rubbing the napkin between her fingers.

'Is something wrong?' he asked when her silence continued.

She pulled her lips in together, colour heightening across her cheekbones, then took a number of deep breaths.

'Freya?'

'Can I have a glass of wine, please?' she said quietly. 'There is something I need to tell you.'

Apprehension filling him, he took the bottle from the ice bucket and filled her glass.

She took a large sip then set the glass on the table, clutching the stem in her hand.

Then she took another deep breath and squared her shoulders before squaring her jaw. 'My mother is ill. The house in London is not for me. It's for her. For both of them.'

Now Benjamin was the one to take a long drink of his wine.

'What is wrong with her?' he asked, already

knowing from her tone and the serious hue reflecting from her eyes that it was not good.

He watched the signs of her faltering composure, the fluttering of the hand not clinging to her glass, the rapid rise and fall of her chest, the movement of her throat.

'She has a rare degenerative neurological disease that affects muscle movement. There is no cure.'

Banging immediately set off in his head. 'No cure…?'

'It's terminal,' she supplied matter-of-factly but with the slightest cracking of her voice on the final syllable.

Benjamin swore under his breath, a clammy feeling crawling over his skin.

'I want her to end her days in a home that has space and with a garden she can sit out in and listen to the birds and feel the breeze on her face.'

'I understand that,' he said heavily.

Her smile when she met his eyes was sad. 'I know you do.'

His heart ached in a way it hadn't done in seven years, the beats dense and weighty. 'Is there *nothing* that can be done for her?'

'There has been a medical development in America recently, a treatment that slows it down in some cases and in even rarer cases reverses some of the symptoms. Not permanently though. No one has found a permanent reversal.'

Everything suddenly became clear.

Pushing his unfinished plate to one side, Benjamin rubbed his temples. 'That's why you married me. To pay for the treatment.'

'Yes.' She shuffled her chair back a little and stretched her neck. 'It's not authorised for use in the UK because it's unproven and incredibly expensive. The money I get from our marriage is to pay for her to have a doctor fly to England every month and administer it to her in a private hospital. It won't keep her alive for ever, but it might give us an extra year or two, and they could be good years for her. The money Javier paid after we signed the contract on our engagement has paid for two cycles of it. Her speech and breathing have improved a little and she's got slightly more movement in her hands. It's stopped it getting any worse. For now,' she added with a sigh. 'None of us are stupid enough to think it will hold it off for ever.'

'Miracles do happen.' But his words were automatic. Miracles were something he had stopped believing in during his mother's battle with cancer.

Freya shook her head ruefully. 'Not for my mother. When the treatment is developed more in the future they might be able to fully reverse it and hold the symptoms off permanently but that will come way too late for Mum. We're just grateful that she's receiving *any* benefit from it. She's already proving to be one of the lucky rare ones.'

Lucky to be trapped in a failing body with no hope of lasting longer than a year or two?

'And now I can give them a home too.' She paused and blinked rapidly. 'I never told them. I was scared to jinx it. They've wanted to move for years. They live in a two-bedroom third-floor flat in a building with communal gardens that are used by the local drug addicts. They're basically prisoners in their own home now.'

'We can fly to London tomorrow to look at the houses.'

She blinked again, this time in astonishment. 'Don't you have to work?'

'Some things are more important. We can fly out after breakfast.'

He saw her throat move. 'That is incredibly generous of you. Thank you.'

'If I had known why you wanted a house I would have made it a priority.'

'I didn't think you'd care.'

He winced at her unflinching honesty. 'I cannot say I blame you for that.'

'It wasn't just that I didn't think you'd care,' she said in a softer, more reflective tone. 'I'm not good at opening up in any capacity, especially about such personal matters.'

'Your dance does your talking for you.'

For a moment she just stared at him, eyes glistening before she jerked a nod. 'It's the only way I know how. I find it hard opening up at the best of times. I didn't want to share something so personal with someone I hated.'

He hesitated before asking, 'Does that mean you no longer hate me?'

'I don't know.' She took a sip of her wine. 'You're not the complete monster I thought you were. You had your reasons to do what you did. I feel a certain…kinship, I think the word is. I understand what you were going through when your mother was ill because I'm living it myself. You signed a contract without reading the terms and conditions; I signed a contract pledging my life in exchange for an extension to hers. If that makes me a gold-digger then I can live with that.'

He closed his eyes briefly and breathed heavily. 'You are not a gold-digger. I should never have called you that.'

She shrugged, her shoulders tight. 'It doesn't matter. You could have called me worse.'

He'd thought worse. When he recalled the things he had thought about her he wanted to retch. She had married him to extend her mother's life. He had married her out of vengeance against his oldest friend.

'It does matter. I know what it's like to watch someone you love slowly lose their life. You will do anything to help them and give them more time.'

Their eyes met. Something, a flash of understanding, passed between them that, like a switch being flicked, darkened and deepened.

He blew out a long puff of air and got to his feet. 'We'll make an early start tomorrow. Get some sleep and I will see you in the morning.'

There was a smattering of confusion in her returning stare before she nodded. 'See you in the morning.'

CHAPTER TWELVE

THE FAMILIAR RATTLE of the cattle grid woke Freya from the sleep she had fallen into. Covering a yawn with her hand, she cast a quick glance at Benjamin beside her. His face was glued to his laptop as it had been since they'd got into the car from the heliport. The seductive looks and words were a thing of the past.

She felt as if she had lived a thousand lives in the past two days.

They had spent the day in London as he had promised. He'd organised everything. A stretched Mercedes had met them at the airport with Giles, Benjamin's assistant who had been tasked with house-hunting for her, in attendance, and then driven them to all the shortlisted houses.

She had fallen in love with the second property, which ticked every box she'd wanted and more.

Best of all, it was unoccupied.

Benjamin had made an immediate cash offer and got the wheels put into motion for the quickest of quick sales. Her parents could move in that coming weekend. Benjamin was going to take care of everything for them.

He had then taken her to the tower block her parents lived in but had refused to come in with her.

'This is a home you are providing for them,' he had explained without looking at her. 'It is better they hear it from you. I will only be a distraction.'

'But they will want to meet you,' she had said, surprising herself with her own argument. 'They will want to thank you.'

His nose had wrinkled before he'd looked at the building she had called home for the first eleven years of her life. 'There will be plenty of time for us to meet in the future. I have things to organise. Giles will see you in. Take all the time you need. There is no rush.'

She had then spent a wonderful couple of hours with her parents, finally having the confidence to tell them they were going to be able to move out of the flat that had become their prison into a house of their own, and that her new husband was in the process of getting a team together to help them make the move and would be providing them with an unlimited credit card to furnish their new home to their liking.

Javier had been prepared to buy them a home as part of the contract. He had known about their situation for two whole months.

Benjamin had known about it for less than a day

and had already gone above and beyond his contractual obligations.

And yet there was a distance between them that had never been there before. He had hardly looked her in the eye all day. And it had been a long day, dinner eaten in silence on the return flight back to Provence.

'It is late,' he said as the car came to a stop in the courtyard. 'I am going to call it a night.'

'You're going to bed?' she asked, surprised at the stab of disappointment cutting through her stomach.

'I have a few more calls to make and then I will sleep. I'll see you in the morning. *Bonne nuit.*'

And that was that.

The man who had devoured her with his eyes, who had insisted they would sleep together every night they were under the same roof, would be sleeping in his own bed without her for the second night in a row.

Feeling nauseous although she had no idea why, Freya carried her heavy legs up the stairs.

It *was* late. Maybe she should get some sleep too.

But after taking a shower and brushing her teeth she knew sleep was a long way off. There was a knotted feeling in her stomach that time was only making worse.

All she could think was that Benjamin was bored of her after only one night together.

Or, worse, had her confession about her family background turned him off? Had seeing the place she had been raised tainted her somehow too? Did he see her differently now he knew her polish and poise had been taught and were not inherent in her?

And why did her heart hurt so much to think all this?

She shouldn't care. She should be thankful his desire for her had been turned off. Wasn't that the safety she craved where all her passion and emotions were expressed in her dance?

The knot in her stomach tightened, pulling at her chest, and she paced her room until she could take no more and, uncaring that it was the middle of the night, bolted out of her quarters.

Thoughts and questions crowding her head, her heart throbbing, she hurried up the stairs to her studio and threw her dressing gown on the floor. Not wanting to waste time putting on tights and a leotard, she pulled a black, calf-length floating exercise dress off the rail in the studio cupboard and shrugged it over her head.

The pointe shoes she had softened into reasonable comfort the day before were on the floor where she had left them and still had plenty of wear left. She put them on, tied the ribbons, then put the sound system on shuffle and settled herself by her barre.

Inhaling deeply through her nose, she then exhaled through her mouth and repeated ten times, determined to clear her mind while stretching her limbs and increasing her blood flow.

But as she made the familiar comforting movements, her eyes drifted around the studio.

Everything that had been done to create this had been with one focus in mind—her needs. The light she needed. The height she needed. The space she needed. Nothing had been missed, nothing stinted on.

The music she had been stretching to came to an end and seconds later the opening bars to the Habanera from *Carmen* came on in its stead.

Freya paused as the wonderful score, with its seductive Spanish vibe, filled the studio.

The Habanera was the part where the immoral, wicked Carmen danced with such allure that Don José, the soldier about to arrest her, instead fell for the temptress and bedded her.

It was a most sensual of dances and, though she had danced it many times, Freya had never wriggled her shoulders at the start and imagined a real, flesh and blood man watching her and desiring her for real.

Had Carmen desired Don José when she had danced for him? Freya had always assumed not, thought of the dance as a trap to hook him in— one that obviously backfired considering he killed her at the end for loving another man—but now, as

Benjamin's features shone brightly in front of her, the dance moves coming back to her, she wondered if in the heat of the moment Carmen *had* felt desire for the man she used for her own ends.

Maybe that was all it was for her and Benjamin too, a desire born through circumstance that now, in Benjamin's case, was spent.

She wished with all her heart that it were spent in herself too but it had only grown. Benjamin had made love to her and only now, as she made a series of jetés across the perfect floor, did she acknowledge the truth to herself that every part of her body ached for him to touch her and make love to her again.

She wished he were there with her right now, that she could pirouette to him and see that hunger in his eyes again.

Benjamin could hear music.

At first he'd thought he was imagining it but there was an echoing, haunting sound ringing through the chateau's thick walls, usually so still and silent in the dead of night.

He looked up at the ceiling.

Freya's studio was directly above his own quarters.

He closed his eyes.

He hadn't slept well the night before. Two bad nights' sleep had left him exhausted.

Three large Scotches in quick succession meant he should have passed out the moment his head hit the pillow but he couldn't even shut his eyes without forcing them.

He opened them again and stared at the ceiling. The heavy beat of his heart echoed in his ears and he put a hand to his bare chest in an attempt to temper it.

All he wanted was to go to her. All he wanted was to haul her into his arms and make love to her, again and again.

He'd spent the day with her avoiding her gaze, knowing that to look into those black depths would pull him back into a place he needed to keep away from.

His head was a whirl of diverging thoughts but the one that flashed loudest was that he should never have married her. If he had known about her mother and her parents' situation he would have paid her off when she'd suggested it rather than tie her into this.

Wouldn't he…?

Yes, he *would* have paid her off, he told himself forcefully. Freya hadn't pledged herself to Javier for her own greedy benefit as he had assumed. None of it had been for herself.

Why wasn't she sleeping? Her conscience was clear. There was nothing to stop her sleeping as sweetly as he had always been able to do.

But she was awake and dancing above him.

Freya needed to dance in the same way he needed air. There was still so much to learn about her but on the very essence of who she was he had no doubts.

Dieu, he ached to see her, hold her, kiss her, touch her...

She was all he had wanted since he had seen her that first time with the sunlight pouring onto her skin.

Benjamin had pulled his trousers back on and reached his bedroom door before even realising he was out of his bed.

With long strides he climbed the stairs and opened the door to her studio.

She was at the far side by the window, moving like a graceful blur to the beats of the music.

There was only the merest glint of surprise when she caught his eye in the reflection of the walled mirror but no pause or hesitation in her movements.

She continued to dance, contorting her body and creating shapes out of her legs and arms that appeared completely natural and effortless. She'd left her hair loose and it flew around her, spinning in a perfect wheel when she spun on pointe, all the while her eyes seeming to never leave his.

And he could not tear his eyes from her.

He had never, in his entire life, been witness to anything so beautiful or seductive.

Freya didn't dance, she *was* dance; she was the emotion of the music brought to life. She was incredible.

Closer and closer she came, every fluid motion bringing her nearer to him until she jumped with her left leg fully extended and her right leg bent at the knee, creating the illusion of flight.

She landed a foot before him and sank into a bow.

Slowly she raised herself back up to stare at him with a stillness that was as elegant and stunning as her movement.

She didn't speak.

He didn't speak.

They just gazed at each other.

It felt as if her eyes were piercing right into his soul.

And then she flew at him.

At least that was how it seemed in the moment, that she had taken flight to throw her arms around his neck and her supple legs around his waist, holding and supporting herself around him without any effort.

Benjamin gazed at the perfection of her face for one more moment before all the pent-up desire and emotions inside him burst free.

Wrapping his arms tightly around her back, he crushed his lips to hers and was met with her matching hunger. Like two starving waifs finally being given a meal, they kissed greedily and possessively, his hands splaying and digging into her back, her fingers digging into the nape of his neck, fusing every part of their bodies together they could.

His arousal, a simmering feature of his life he had learned to endure since he'd stolen her out of the hotel and her hand had first slipped into the crook of his arm, burned. Everything in him burned, from the lava in his veins to the swirling molten heat of his skin.

From the heat of Freya's kisses and the tightness of her legs around him, he knew it was the same for her too.

This was a need too great and too explosive to do anything but quench. The sensual music only added to the mixture, creating the most potent chemical cocktail that, now ignited, had only one possible outcome.

With nowhere to lay her down, Benjamin carried her effortlessly to the nearest wall and slammed her against it.

Slipping a hand up the skirt of her dress, which had bunched up against the top of her toned thighs, he found her bottom deliciously bare, and pressed his palm to the damp heat of her pubis.

She gasped into his mouth and pressed against him, unhooking an arm from his neck to drop it down to his waist and the band of his trousers.

Until she dug her hand into the opening, he

hadn't realised he hadn't buttoned himself up. Like her, he was naked beneath the only item of clothing he wore. She caressed him, biting into his bottom lip with her teeth before sweeping her tongue back into his mouth and kissing him harder than ever.

He grabbed her hand with his and, together, they pulled him free. With no further restrictions, all that was left was to adjust their forms against the wall until he was there, fully hard and fully ready, and thrusting up into her welcome tightness.

There was no savouring of the moment, not from either of them. The instant he was fully inside her, Freya's hand grabbed his buttocks and she was urging him on with her body and with mumbled, indecipherable words.

Their lovemaking had a primal, almost feral quality to it, he thought dimly as he thrust into her. Her nails now dug into his skin as she matched him, thrust for thrust, stroke for stroke, until the hand still on his neck suddenly grabbed at his hair and she cried out, every part of her clenching around him in a spasm that seemed to go on for ever and pulled him even tighter inside her and then he, too, could hold on no more and he let go as the most powerful climax of his life ripped through him.

Freya stretched out her leg and immediately her foot connected with something solid and warm and very, very human. Benjamin's leg.

Her languid limbs wakened properly as all that had gone on between them through the night came back to her like a glorious cinematic masterpiece in her head.

The ghost dream had come to life. She had danced to her lover. She had danced *for* her lover.

Her *lover*.

How else could she describe him after they had come together like two people possessed?

After the explosion that had rocked them in his studio, he had carried her down to his bedroom and made love to her all over again.

And she had made love to him too.

The song birds were already singing the dawn chorus when they finally sated their hunger.

Incredibly, the familiar ache in her loins fired up again. The hunger hadn't been sated, merely put to sleep.

She could handle this, she thought as she snuggled closer to him. A huge arm hooked around her and in an instant she was wrapped back in the wonderful comfort of Benjamin's strong body, his warm skin smelling of them and the heat they had created between these sheets.

This was no big deal. This was merely two compatible people who happened to be married unlocking their desire for each other.

It didn't mean anything. It didn't affect anything. The rest of their contract would stay the same.

Nothing else would change because of it.

It couldn't. She wouldn't let it.

She would not let these wonderful feelings erupt into anything more.

The risks were far too great.

'No, no, no, *jeté* to the *left*! Freya, *concentrate*!'

'I'm sorry.' Freya stopped moving and put her hands on her hips, leaning forward and breathing in deeply. She was exhausted. The rehearsal had started off badly and gone downhill from there. And it was all her fault.

Mikael, the dancer she was supposed to be *jeté*-ing to before pirouetting into his arms, glared at her. The four members of the *corps de ballet* merely looked embarrassed.

The harassed choreographer sighed. 'Let's take a fifteen-minute break. Come back with heads screwed on.'

Freya went straight to her dressing room. She drank some water and ate a banana, then went back to the studio determined to get it right.

The rest of the rehearsal was even worse. She couldn't even get the basic footwork right and these were moves she had been doing since she was a small child. It was as if her feet no longer connected to her brain and her arms were made of modelling clay.

She returned to her apartment knowing one more

bad rehearsal could mean her understudy being given the role of Vicky.

This was a role she had coveted for so long and she was in danger of losing it. Every dancer had a bad day but this had been a bad week, following on from a week that had been only marginally better.

Her dancing was deteriorating and she could not for the life of her think why.

She had one more day to get through and then she had a day off. If she could get through the next day's rehearsals she would then have time away to recharge and refocus her mind.

She checked her phone as she ran a bath and found a message from her father, his daily update.

She read it and closed her eyes with the first smile to cross her lips all week.

At least here was some good news. Her mother had wiggled all the fingers of her left hand and hummed along to a song on the radio.

Her mood managed to lighten even more before plunging when her phone rang in her hand and Benjamin's name flashed on the screen.

'*Bonsoir, ma douce.*' The rich seductiveness of his tone sent tingles of sensation curling across her spine.

'Hi.'

'Is everything okay?' he asked.

'Yes. All good.'

She would not admit her body was forgetting

the basic dance moves that had been ingrained in her before she'd learned her times tables. As far as Benjamin was concerned, everything was fine.

He hated her being back in Madrid. It was a simple, mostly unspoken truth between them and she knew it was a proprietorial thing for him. Benjamin hated his wife working for his enemy.

And she hated it too. Mercifully, she hadn't seen anything of Javier or Luis since she had arrived back to work but she found herself constantly on alert for them, which she knew was stupid as Javier especially rarely bothered to grace them with his presence.

Mercifully too, the new building the company had moved into, adjacent to the new theatre that was undergoing its finishing touches, meant her fellow dancers had been too busy exploring and comparing to bother with her. Freya jilting Javier for Benjamin was already old news. There had been the odd snide comment, of course, but the kind she had inured herself against over a decade ago. It grieved her deeply that Sophie had unexpectedly quit the company and returned to England but what she hated the most, and which she also would never admit, was that her mind was almost completely occupied with Benjamin.

Freya had known that keeping a lid on her feelings for him would be hard, especially after they had become proper lovers, but she had never imagined the strength it would take to keep that lid on. He called her every night, and she would listen to the rich honeyed tones with an ache in her heart that had slipped into her every pore.

She did *not* miss him, she told herself constantly. And she did *not* count down the hours until she would be with him again.

But the precipice she had seen her mother edging towards if she didn't accept his proposal was now inching towards her. She could feel it with every minute spent with him and every communication between them, a drop of unimaginable depths waiting to swallow her whole if she couldn't keep her feet rooted to the ground and that lid on, even if she needed to pull it down with both hands gripped tightly to it.

The days they had spent together as lovers before she had left for Madrid had been the best days of her life.

They had spent most of them in bed, yes, but they had enjoyed themselves out of it too. He had joined her in her studio while she practised, making calls and sending emails with her pirouetting around him. They had eaten their separate meals together and even shared more of the same meals. They had shared stories of their childhoods, very different but fascinating to the other.

And then they had flown to England together and met her parents in their new house.

He had been welcomed with open arms and even wider hearts.

And then she had gone back to her life and found everything had changed.

She had changed.

'*Bien.* I just want to check you have no late re-hearsals tomorrow.' It was only when she heard him speak after days apart that she heard the thickness of his accent when he spoke her language. She never heard it when she was with him any more.

'Not that I've been told.'

'*Excellente.* I will get my driver to collect you at six-thirty.'

A few minutes later, Freya disconnected the call and climbed into the huge bath.

Then she laid herself down until she was fully submerged and held her breath for as long as she could.

CHAPTER THIRTEEN

FREYA RAN A brush through her hair a final time and laid it on her dresser feeling much better in herself. Rehearsals the day before had gone much better. Today, after a night of making love to Benjamin, she had taken herself to her studio to practise her solo dance and found herself foot-perfect. Not a single step or movement had been wrong, and she had dressed for their night out feeling as if a weight had been lifted.

Now she could enjoy a meal out with her husband without any cares.

Selecting a red button-down shirt-dress that fell to her knees, a thick black rope belt hooked around her waist and a pair of high strappy silver sandals, she then dabbed perfume behind her ears and on her wrists, applied a little gloss to her lips and considered herself done.

She found Benjamin in the half-inside, half-outside living room where he had first told her she would have to marry him, talking on his phone.

He got to his feet when he saw her and ended his call.

Tilting his head, he studied her with sparkling eyes.

'Madame Guillem, you look good enough to eat.'

The feeling is entirely mutual, she thought but didn't say.

Charcoal trousers, a shirt only a shade lighter and unbuttoned at his throat, and a Prussian blue jacket gave him a dangerously debonair appearance.

'Where are we going?' she asked.

'I've booked us a table at Le Cheval D'Or.'

'Where's that?'

'A restaurant near Nice. It's about half an hour's drive away.'

When they stepped out in the courtyard Benjamin smiled to see the furrow on Freya's brow at the car waiting for them, a bright yellow convertible with the roof down.

She ran her fingers along the paintwork and then suddenly that striking face was grinning widely. 'What a beautiful car.'

'It's a 1949 Buick Roadmaster Riviera Convertible. I bought it at auction four months ago.'

She stepped all around it, examining it with the same reverence he'd first studied it. When she was done, he opened the passenger door for her.

Her brow furrowed again. 'Where's your driver?'

He grinned. 'Tonight, *ma douce*, *I* am your driver.'

She matched his grin and got in.

Minutes later, they were out of his estate and speeding through the sweeping roads to their destination, Freya's hair sweeping around her.

'This is amazing,' she said, bursting into laughter, a sound he had never heard from her before.

As incredible as it was to believe, he had never heard Freya laugh until that moment.

Her joy was as infectious as it was heart-warming and he laughed with her. 'Isn't it?'

Not much more was said but every time he looked at her she would turn her eyes to him and they would give identical grins.

Benjamin was big enough to admit he was greedy about his time with her. Since she had returned to Madrid he guarded their time together zealously. He wanted her to be happy but seven hours in her studio on her one whole day off?

He'd resented ballet enough for stealing all his mother's attention while she was alive and now he found himself with a wife whose passion for it would more commonly be known as an addiction.

He reflected that next week she had two whole days off. He'd already rearranged his diary to free his time so they didn't have to waste any of it.

Tonight he had deliberately booked a table in a restaurant rather than dine at home as they usually did. Selfishly, he wanted all her attention.

So far his ploy was working.

Ten minutes from the restaurant and the first clear view of the Mediterranean appeared; he looked at her and laughed again to see her head flopping on her shoulder.

'You're falling asleep?' he asked with faux incredulity.

She straightened and gave a yawn that turned into muffled giggles. 'Sorry... Wow! That view is incredible.'

All sleepiness deserted her in an instant as Freya took in the glamorous sight in front of them, so different from the peaceful views that surrounded Benjamin's chateau but equally beautiful in its own right.

But none of those views were a patch on the masculine beauty of the man who sat beside her, driving a car that wouldn't look out of place in one of those glamourous films from the Cary Grant era. It suited Benjamin perfectly, far more than any modern-day Bugatti or Ferrari, cars she knew he had in his underground garage.

The wind whipping through her hair and the feel of the sun soaking into her face had rid her of the last of that godawful tightness that had been compressing her all week.

This was *fun*.

She honestly could not remember the last time she had done anything that constituted fun. Maybe the theme park she and Sophie had visited on one of their days off on their European tour last year? They hadn't gone this year. Sophie had begged off with stomach cramps and Freya hadn't wanted to go without her.

She wished she knew what was wrong with her oldest and closest friend and why she had quit the company so abruptly, but Sophie had clammed up.

Soon the roads became even narrower and steeper and they drove into a town with medieval architecture, coming to a stop outside a high monastic stone building with a red-tiled roof and pillars.

Immediately a valet appeared, opening the passenger door for her and helping her out, then zipping to Benjamin's side. Benjamin pressed the keys in the valet's hand then turned to Freya with a grin. 'Ready?'

'Ready.'

Stone walls and floors greeted them, along with high stained-glass windows and a high vaulted ceiling. A low buzz of chatter rang out from the other diners, all dressed in their finery, low bursts and high bursts of laughter and the most delicious smells.

They were led to a table under a window, menus presented to them by the self-important maître d' with the same reverence as if they were being presented with a first edition of a masterpiece. He then took hold of their napkins and, in turn, flicked them to open them up, his face grave as if performing an act of live art as he placed them on their laps.

Freya caught the laughter in Benjamin's eye and ducked her head down to study the menu lest she start giggling at the maître d's pomposity.

The second he left their table, they covered their mouths so the laughter they'd both been supressing came out like muffled sniggers.

'Were we supposed to applaud?' she said when she'd caught her breath, dabbing a tear of mirth with the napkin.

'I think he expected a standing ovation.'

By the time they'd ordered their food—thankfully their order was taken by one of the lowly waiters—Freya felt thoroughly relaxed and sipped her champagne with pleasure.

The food they were served was incredible, her starter of artichoke served with caviar in a lime broth possibly the best dish she had ever eaten... until their main courses were set before them and she had her first bite of her clay-cooked chicken that came with white asparagus, a rocket salad and little delicacies she didn't recognise but knew would be delicious.

'I have never seen you enjoy your food so much,' Benjamin commented as he tackled his smoked lobster. 'I must get my chef to recreate these recipes.'

'Your chef is amazing,' she protested. 'I'm just exceptionally hungry.'

'So am I.'

Her heart leapt at the gleam in his eyes and the suggestiveness of his tone, sending a hot surge of blood pumping through her.

Would this desire ever abate?

His sparkling eyes devouring her a little longer, he said, 'It is strange to see you eat a meal out without worrying over every ingredient.'

She laughed. 'I allow myself the occasional splurge. I've only had one non-healthy meal since you kidnapped me and that was on our wedding day.'

'You hardly ate any of that and I didn't kidnap you. I whisked you away with deception.'

'If it looks like a duck, walks like a duck and talks like a duck then it's safe to say it's a duck. You kidnapped me.'

'Ducks can't talk and I didn't kidnap you.'

'Okay, you stole me, then.'

'Only with your consent, and ask yourself this—who would you rather be sitting at this table with? Me or Javier?'

'You want me to answer that?'

He flashed her a grin that didn't quite meet his eyes. 'Only if the answer is me.'

It's you, every time, she almost said but cut herself off.

She couldn't lie to him but nor could she tell him the truth.

Instinct told her that to tell the truth would be to drag her even closer to the precipice that frightened her so much.

She never thought of Javier unless it was to compare him unfavourably to Benjamin.

Her brain burned to remember she had agreed to have children with him. The ball had been entirely in her court as to when it would happen so she had decided that she would wait until her biological clock started ticking, thinking by then she and Javier would have forged a friendly marriage.

She no longer believed anything of the sort. How could she when she now believed the heart she'd thought he kept hidden from view was actually missing? The way he and Luis had treated Benjamin and taken advantage of his mother's cancer for their own ends enraged her.

Benjamin's heart wasn't missing. His heart was as enormous as his ego. He was a man who did everything wholeheartedly, whether it was loving someone or hating them. When he set on a path he was relentless until he reached his destination.

They had never spoken of children. It was there in the contract though. The ball would always be in her court for that.

What kind of a father would he be? A hands-on, nappy-changing, kicking-a-ball-around-the-park dad? Or the kind of father who appointed an army of nannies and left them to it?

And why did her heart ache to imagine it…?

'You and Javier are very different people,' she said quietly, trying to be diplomatic without giving anything of her thoughts away. 'When I agreed to marry him I knew he was a cold fish but I didn't realise what a complete bastard he was. It wouldn't have changed my mind though. His proposal was just too attractive for my mother's sake.'

'And what about your sake?'

'I have dealt with colder and crueller people than Javier Casillas. You want to know real cruelty, put a hidden camera in a girls' boarding school.'

'Did you suffer a lot?'

'The other girls took an instant dislike to me. They hated everything about me. The clothes I wore, the way I spoke…even the way I held my cutlery. They took pleasure in humiliating me. Petty, nasty things. Constant name calling, stealing my stuff, tripping me in the canteen when I had a tray of food in my hand—that one was a particular favourite.'

'They hated that you were a better dancer than them?'

Her brow furrowed in surprise.

He explained his thinking with a grimace. 'You had a full scholarship. The school you went to only gives them rarely, for exceptional talents.'

She pulled a rueful face. 'If that was their reasoning then it worked. My dancing went to pieces. That first term I was the worst dancer there because they got into my head. I was an insecure bag of nerves.'

'How did you get through it?' But he already had a good idea. That iron control had started somewhere.

'At the end of the first term one of the dance teachers pulled me aside. She told me I was in danger of losing my scholarship. She also said she knew I had problems fitting in but that, unless I wanted to lose my dream, I had to rise above it and find a way to tune the noise out otherwise they would win.'

She would have been only eleven, Benjamin thought, sickened at the cruelty of children and the ineffectiveness of the adults meant to protect her.

'I took her words to heart,' Freya continued. 'I taught myself to block the noise from my head and focus only on the dance itself. I no longer sought their approval and in time I no longer wanted or needed it. By taking control of my feelings and learning to be completely single-minded, I learned how to survive.' Her face brightened a touch. 'And I did make a friend eventually. Sophie. She helped ease the loneliness but they were still the worst days of my life. If I could get through that, I can get through anything. If marrying Attila the Hun could have alleviated my mother's pain I would have married him and known I would survive it too.'

Benjamin saw so many emotions flickering in the black depths of her eyes that his heart fisted in on itself.

Their backgrounds might have them poles apart but when it came to those they loved, there was nothing either of them would not do.

Having met her parents for himself, he understood even more.

He had been struck with the warmth of their welcome, their gratitude for the home he had given them so stark it had embarrassed him.

It isn't me you need to thank, he'd wanted to tell them. *It's your daughter. She's the one who contracted herself out to marriage for you.*

He'd thought he'd been prepared for her mother's condition but it had been worse than he'd thought. She could do nothing for herself, was virtually paralysed in her failing body, totally reliant on her doting husband. And Freya said this was an improvement?

But she had that spirit in her eyes his own mother had had, a will to fight, and, he had seen whenever she had looked at her only child, fierce pride in her daughter.

Strangely, meeting Freya's father, a humble man with a huge heart, had set him thinking about his own when he so rarely thought of his own father.

The only good thing his father had ever done—apart from helping create himself and his sister, even if he did say so himself—was provide maintenance to his mother once he'd left the family nest. His mother had saved all those payments, giving Benjamin his share in a lump sum when he'd turned twenty-one, money he'd used to purchase an old, run-down food-production facility.

He'd left his in-laws' home with a heavy heart, which he still hadn't shaken off.

'How can you stand working for him?' he asked.

Javier had known about her mother's condition for two months and done nothing about it other than sign promises for the future when he had his ring on Freya's finger.

Yes, he had paid for two rounds of treatment but he should have taken them out of that decrepit flat and given them somewhere decent to live.

'I don't work for him. I work for his company,' she answered. 'And it won't be for much longer.'

'Have you started looking for a new company yet?'

'I've been approached by a couple of companies.'

'You never said.'

'My career is not your concern,' she reminded him with a tight smile that immediately made his hackles rise.

'I spoke to the director of Orchestre National de Paris a few days ago,' he said. 'Their theatre has just been refurbished and the owner is in the process of creating a new ballet company.'

'I am aware of that.'

'They want you to be their Etoile.'

'What?'

'Orchestre National de Paris want you to be the star of their new ballet company. I was going to wait until the proposal was confirmed in writing before telling you but now seems the right time. Salary is negotiable and they are prepared to put a clause in your contract that allows you time off to guest star for other companies.'

Silence filled the space between them. She stared at him, totally still, her black eyes unreadable.

'Who approached who?' she asked slowly. 'You or the director?'

'Does it matter?'

'Yes.'

'The director is an old friend who I know through the Casillas brothers. The Orchestre National de Paris's intention to create its own ballet company is not a secret.'

An edge crept into her voice. 'But who approached who?'

'I called him.'

'Did you call him with the intention of pimping me out?'

Anger, already simmering in his guts, cut through him. He controlled it. Just. 'Having a conversation to get my wife a better deal with a better company is hardly pimping.'

She leaned forward ever so slightly. 'And who are you to say what is a better deal for me? Or which is the better company?'

'You are a dancer whose star is in the ascendancy. This move will help you reach the pinnacle that much more quickly.'

'And how will it look when people find out I only got the job thanks to my husband being part of the old boys' network with the director?'

'I don't know that term but I can guess what it means, and no one is going to think that because it is not true.'

'Did you not listen to a single word I just said? Everything I have achieved has been on my own merits and I have worked my toes into stumps to get where I am, without *any* help. What makes you think I need help with my career now? And who the *hell* do you think you are, interfering like this?'

'Interfering?' He was taken aback at her venom. 'I am your husband. It is my job to look out for you.'

'It is *not*. My career is entirely separate to our marriage and you have overstepped the mark hugely.'

How he kept his temper he would never know. 'I am sorry you feel I have overstepped your invisible mark but I am sick of living in a separate country to my wife. I *am* your husband. You married me and took my name. I have an apartment in Paris. Take the job and we can live there when you are working and have a proper marriage.'

There. His cards were on the table.

He stared hard at her waiting for her to respond.

'It's not an invisible mark. It's in the contract we both signed. No interference in my career.' Her voice contained the slightest of tremors.

'If you want us to stick to the contract then answer this—if I were to take advantage of the clause that said I could take a mistress, how would it make you feel?'

Her face turned the colour of chalk. Her throat moved numerous times before she whispered, 'I wouldn't try to stop you.'

'I didn't ask if you would try to stop me. I asked how it would make you feel.'

'I would accept it.'

'Accept it?' he sneered.

'I signed up for a marriage that allows us both to live an independent life and I don't want to change any of it. If I move to Paris it will be because that's what's right for my career.' She took a long sip of champagne and blew out a long puff of air before saying, 'I *do* appreciate you thinking of me. I will speak to the director of Orchestre National de Paris but I'm not going to make any promises. My career comes first, you already know that.'

Wishing he hadn't chosen to drive, Benjamin jerked a nod.

Why had he thought the outcome of this conversation would be any different?

His own parents had both put him second to their needs. Why should he think his wife would be any different?

The drive back to his chateau was a far more muted affair than the drive to the restaurant, hardly a word exchanged between them.

Twenty minutes after they'd left, right on cue, Freya had fallen asleep. A minute after that, her head fell onto his shoulder and stayed there for the final eight miles.

Benjamin had put the roof back up before setting off and, without the wind to drive it away, her sultry scent filled the enclosed space cocooning them. It was a scent that slowly worked its way into his senses and pushed out the anger that had gripped him at her uncompromising attitude.

As he brought the Buick to a stop, her face made a movement and then she opened her eyes.

She didn't look surprised to find her head resting on his shoulder.

'I fell asleep again,' she whispered, making no attempt to move away from him.

'You did.'

Her black eyes stayed on his, darkening and

swirling. And then she did move, shifting slightly to bring her face closer to his and to brush her lips against his…

Much later, naked and replete in her arms, Benjamin reflected that if fantastic sex was the most he got out of this marriage then he would be a luckier man than most.

If Freya wanted to stick to the exact letter of that damned contract, then so be it. From now on he would stick to the damned thing too.

CHAPTER FOURTEEEN

FREYA WANTED TO scream until all the fear and frustration that held her in its grip was ripped from her.

She settled on crawling into a ball in the corner of the living room and rocking.

She'd thought she'd cracked the role of Vicky.

That afternoon she had walked into the practice room to overhear a seething Mikael shouting at the choreographer that he would not 'partner someone who cares so little for the dance'.

'We can't replace her,' the choreographer had replied with the exasperation of someone who had already had that conversation. 'Her face is *everywhere*. The opening night is a sell-out because of her.'

'She is a terrible dancer.'

'Usually she is the best…'

And then they had noticed her standing at the door, aghast at what she had just heard.

'Freya…' the choreographer had begun, but Mikael had cut him off to barge past her saying loudly for anyone passing to hear, 'You find your dancing feet or you find a new partner. I will not be associated with this crap.'

She couldn't even blame him. She would feel the same if she were lumbered with a partner who had lost all co-ordination and couldn't remember the simplest moves in their dances.

In her studio at the chateau she was foot-perfect.

She *did* know the dances. She knew the whole choreography for the whole production. She just could not translate what was in her head to her feet.

So frightened had she become about it that she'd paid a private doctor to test her for the cruel disease slowly killing her mother.

The fast-tracked results had come back negative.

Whatever was wrong with her was psychological not physiological.

The problem was in her head.

Impulse had her leaping to her feet and flying to her phone.

She would call Benjamin,

Since she had virtually ruined their evening out together by reminding him of the terms of their contract, his daily calls when she was in Madrid had reduced to nothing.

She hadn't meant to anger him but he was breaking the terms of their contract, interfering when he had no business to.

That interference had terrified her but not half as much as his reasons for it had.

He *knew* she couldn't give him a marriage of true spouses. He'd never wanted a true marriage either. This was a marriage he had backed her into a corner to wed herself to and now he was trying to change all the rules. She had given him her name. She had given him her body when she had never thought she would give that to *anyone*. Hadn't he taken enough already?

Why did he have to push things when the career she kept such tight control of was already spinning away from her faster than she could pirouette? And to threaten to take a mistress…?

She would not think about that.

But he *had* called her the other morning as she'd been locking her apartment door to go to work, checking if she would be available to accompany him to a business dinner on her next days off.

She'd found the mere sound of his beautiful voice soothing and that morning's practice had been the best of the whole week.

'Is something the matter?' he asked without pre-amble when he answered.

'No,' she denied automatically. 'What makes you ask?'

'You have never called me before.'

'Oh. I just wanted…' *To hear your voice.* 'To check what I should wear to your business dinner.'

'I would never presume to tell you what to wear, *ma douce*. Come dressed as Carabosse if you want.'

She disconnected the call with ice in her veins.

Carabosse was the wicked fairy godmother in *The Sleeping Beauty*.

The faint sound of music seeped through the ceiling and into Benjamin's office.

It was a sound that wrenched at him, the sound of his wife under his roof but hidden away from him.

On the nights they were together she made love to him with abandon but the days they were apart she treated him with indifference. She never called him or messaged him or made any effort to keep in touch. Her one call to him had been for advice on an outfit. As if he knew anything about women's fashion.

He knew his reaction had been harsh but when he'd seen her name flash up on his phone for the first time in almost seven weeks of marriage, he'd been gripped by fear for her.

Why else would she call unless there was something wrong?

His wife wanted him for two things. Money for her family and sex for herself. As a husband he was surplus to requirements, a fact he was finding harder to deal with as time passed rather than easier.

Come the morning she would be up and showered by six, ready to return to her life in Madrid, the life she refused to include him in.

It should not smart. This was what he'd signed up for. Two separate lives.

But it did.

There was a tap on his office door.

Immediately he straightened in his chair and pressed a key on his computer to spring the unused screen back to life.

'Entrez.'

To his surprise, it was his wife who stepped inside.

'Do you have a minute?' she asked quietly.

She was wearing the black practice dress she'd worn when he had made love to her in her studio for the first time. Hair had sprung free from the loose bun she had pulled it back into, her whole appearance more dishevelled than he had ever seen her be.

The usual stab of lust filled his loins to know that beneath her dress she was completely naked...

He gritted his teeth and turned his attention to his computer screen. 'One moment.'

He used the time to compose himself.

Freya had never graced his office with her presence before.

'What can I do for you?' he asked after making her wait a little longer than was strictly necessary.

She had taken the opportunity to perch herself on his leather sofa, leaning forward with her elbows on her thighs and her hands clasped together.

'I want to ask you a favour.'

'Then ask.'

The black eyes held his before her shoulders dropped and she said, 'I know this is a big ask but will you come to the opening performance on Saturday?'

'I would rather swim with sharks than set foot in a theatre owned by those two bastards.'

'I know you would. I'm not asking this lightly but I could really do with the support.'

He made sure to keep his tone amiable. 'Show me where in the contract it says I have to support you in any way that isn't financial and I will abide by it.'

'I didn't have to go to your business dinner last week.'

'That is hardly the same thing.'

'Please. Benjamin, this is the biggest night of my life.'

'If it is support you require, Javier will be there. I am sure he will be glad to lend his support to you.'

'I would rather swim with sharks than have his support,' she said with a shaky laugh, her words clearly intended as a joke to defuse the tension filling the office.

It had the opposite effect.

'And how would I know that?' he asked silkily.

Her brow furrowed. 'Know what?'

He drummed his fingers on his desk. 'That you

wouldn't want his support. I know nothing of your life outside this chateau. I know nothing of what you do in Madrid. You keep me excluded from it.'

'There's nothing to tell. I go to work, I come home. That's it. That's my life in Madrid.'

'I only have your word for that.'

The furrow turned into grooves. 'What are you implying?'

'You're a clever woman. You can work it out.'

Comprehension glinted in her eyes. 'You're being ridiculous. Do I cross-examine you about your life when we're apart?'

'I spent weeks hoping you would and now I find I do not care that you don't. You are happy to take my money and share my bed but God forbid I want to spend time with you outside our contracted hours or deviate from that contract in any form whatsoever. I had few expectations of what our marriage would be like and the reality is beyond the lowest of them. You are uncompromising and selfish.'

Her mouth dropped open, angry colour staining her face and neck. 'You have the nerve to call me selfish when you *stole* me from another man out of revenge?'

'That *man* and his brother stole over two hundred million euros from me.' The reins of his temper he'd been clinging to finally snapped and he got to his feet, put his hands on his desk and glowered at her. 'You know exactly what they did and now you want me to spend a night under the same roof as them?'

Her entire frame shook, her fingers grasping the material of her dress as if she would rip it to pieces. 'No, I want you to support me. I want you to put *your* selfish, vindictive nature to one side for one night and be there for me.'

'Why do you want my support?' he sneered. 'You don't even want my company. When you're here on your days off you hide yourself away in that damned studio for hours on end.'

'I'm spending hours in there because right now it's the only place I can dance in and remember what I'm supposed to be doing!' Her voice had risen in pitch and she dropped her hold on her dress to clutch at the bundle of hair on the back of her head. 'My dance has gone to pot. My partner hates me, the choreographer is about to have a nervous breakdown and for some reason this chateau is the only place I find my body doing what it's supposed to do. I'm not hiding away from you up there. I'm trying to turn off the noise in my head. I'm terrified that on Saturday night I'm going to step onto the stage and find my feet turned to lead. I'm fighting for my career and you're calling me selfish when all I'm asking is for you to put your vendetta to one side for one night and be there for me. You *owe* me, Benjamin.'

'I do not owe you anything. How long has your dance been suffering?'

'Since I went back to Madrid.'

He stared at her, his heart hardening to stone. 'That's over six weeks. You didn't bother to share any of your worries with me before so why should I care now?'

The coil that had been stretching and stretching the longer this awful conversation had gone on finally snapped and with it the last of Freya's dignity.

Jumping to her feet, she yanked the ruffle holding her bun in place and threw it onto the floor.

'You should care because this is all your fault!' she shouted. '*You've* done this to me. You!'

'How am I responsible for your failure to remember your moves?'

'Because you are! You wanted to know why I was a virgin? Well, this is why! It was the last thing of myself that I could keep for myself, the only thing that wasn't public property. I saw how passion and sex worked, the jealousy and the bitterness, how some dancers threw away their careers because they became blinded and I was scared to open myself up to that. I've worked too hard and my family have made too many sacrifices for me to allow emotions into my life that would distract me from my dance but I had no *idea* how bad it could be. You've got in my head and I can't get you out and it's affecting *everything*! I can only remember the moves properly when I'm here in the chateau with you. If I'm going to have any chance of getting through the performance on Saturday I need...'

'Ask someone else,' he cut in coldly.

'There is no one else!' Fat tears sprang out of her eyes. 'I'm scared, Benjamin. I know you think I'm uncompromising but I don't know how to be any other way. It's the only way I've been able to survive this life. I'm not good at asking for help but I'm asking you because...'

Freya took a deep breath and finally spoke the truth of what lived in her heart, a truth that no amount of denial or putting her fingers in her ears to drown out the noise could deny any longer. 'I need you, Benjamin. I need you. Just you. Even if Mum and Dad and Sophie could all be there I would still need you. So please, I am begging you, for one night, please, put your vendetta aside and be there for me.'

The tightness of his jaw softened, the tight white line he'd pulled his lips into loosening.

And then Freya looked into his eyes and found nothing but enmity.

'*Non.*'

'No?'

'*Non.* I will not be used as an emotional crutch. If it is physical support to retain the dance moves you require I suggest you speak to your choreographer about getting help. If it is emotional support you need then you will have the entire audience on your side and willing you to do well, but I will not be there and I will not be a part of it.'

He spoke as if discussing how to repair a broken car.

The tears that had leaked out of her eyes dried up as comprehension struck home.

Just as she had finally accepted her feelings for him had gone way beyond her control came the stark truth. She had only ever been a tool for him to hurt Javier with.

He didn't care about her.

Her heart splintering into a thousand pieces, fury suddenly cut through the agony and she was filled with the need to hurt him back, to see those stony features flinch and make him feel a fraction of her pain; pain that *he'd* caused.

Right then she hated him more than she'd thought it was possible to hate a living being.

'How many times have you asked me if I would have preferred to have married Javier? I can tell you the answer now. I wish I *had* married him. At least I knew he was a cold emotionless bastard from the off.'

But he didn't flinch. There was not a flicker of emotion to be seen in the icy eyes staring back at her.

He lowered himself back into his seat and folded his arms across his chest.

'Get out.'

She stormed to the door. 'With pleasure.'

'No, I mean get out for good. Pack your things and leave.'

'Are you serious?'

'*Oui, ma douce*, more serious than you could ever comprehend. You are not welcome in my home any more. I should have left you alone to marry Javier. That would have been the best revenge on him, to let him spend his life with Carabosse.'

For an age they stared at each other, all the loathing that had been there at the beginning of their relationship brought back to life for its dying gasps.

'You need to let it go,' she said in as hard a tone as she could muster. 'This vendetta is not going to destroy the Casillas brothers, it's going to destroy you. It's already destroyed your soul.'

Then she walked out of the office, slamming the door behind her.

She was opening the door to her quarters when she heard the most enormous crash ring out from his.

She didn't pause to worry what it could be.

By the time she'd shoved as much of her possessions as she could into her cases, a car and driver were waiting for her in the courtyard.

As she was driven out of the estate she didn't look back.

* * *

Only through iron will did Freya make it through the dress rehearsal.

Her performance was not perfect, not by any stretch of the imagination, but Mikael had only screamed in her face once so the improvement was there.

But she wasn't feeling it. She heard the music but it didn't find her soul the way it always used to do.

Had she lost her soul?

That was a question she had asked herself countless times the last few days.

She had accused Benjamin of having lost his. Had the deal she'd made with the devil caused her to lose hers too?

If he really were the devil then why had he transferred ten million euros into her account the day after he'd thrown her out of his chateau?

Her instinct had been to transfer it straight back but she'd resisted, having the frame of mind to remember her mother.

She had been who he'd transferred the money for. Not Freya.

Benjamin would never let her mother suffer out of spite for Freya because, fundamentally, he was a decent man.

A decent man who had been crossed by his closest friends.

She had asked him to sit in the theatre owned by

the men who had caused so much damage to him, when she knew how much he hated them.

She lay back on the huge bed he had never seen let alone shared with her and put a hand to her chest to still her racing heart, her thought drifting to Vicky Page, the role she would perform to the public for the first time tomorrow night. *The Red Shoes* was a fabulous, iconic production but Freya had spent so long learning the choreography and then frantically working to retain it that the story-line itself had passed her by.

Or had she wilfully blocked it out because of the parallels with her own life…?

The story, in its essence, was about ambition. In it, Vicky, a ballerina starring in her first lead role, finds herself torn, forced to choose between love and her career.

Freya had chosen career over everything since before she had developed breasts.

Vicky chose love.

Vicky made the wrong choice.

Freya feared she had made the wrong choice too.

She had fought against letting Benjamin into her heart from the beginning because the danger had been there right from the very first look between them in Javier's garden. She had pushed against it and fought and fought but all that fight had been for nothing.

Everything she had feared about marrying Benjamin had come to bear. That pull she had felt towards him from that very first glance had grown too strong. Without him she had become untethered, as if her anchor had been sliced away and she were drifting out to sea without a way of steering herself back to land.

If it looked like a duck, talked like a duck and walked like a duck then it was a duck. That was what she had said to him.

'Ducks can't talk,' he'd retorted.

No, ducks couldn't talk, but fools could fall in love even when it was the very worst thing they should do, and she was the biggest fool of all.

Benjamin hadn't just stolen her body, he'd stolen her heart.

She didn't just need him. She loved him.

She'd fallen in love with every vengeful, cruel, generous, thoughtful part of him and to deny it any longer would be like denying the duck its existence.

And now her greatest fear about falling in love had come to bear too. Her dancing had gone to pieces. That was why the music no longer worked its magic in her soul, she realised. She'd given her heart and soul to Benjamin.

The music no longer worked its magic without the man who thought she was the reincarnation of the wicked Carabosse.

CHAPTER FIFTEEN

BENJAMIN CLICKED HIS pen moodily. He'd read the news article spread out on the table before him so many times he could recite it.

A burst of something suddenly pummelled him and he grabbed the offending newspaper, scrunched it into a tight ball and threw it on the floor at the exact moment one of his maids appeared to clear away his breakfast coffee.

She looked at him for a moment then walked straight back out again.

He didn't blame her. He hadn't been in the best of moods lately and was aware of it affecting his entire household.

That didn't stop him getting up from his seat and kicking the ball of paper.

He would tell Pierre he no longer needed to send someone into town to collect him a newspaper any more. Who even read their news in this old-fashioned format any more anyway? It was all there on the Internet, news from all corners of the globe available at his fingertips.

If he stopped getting it he could avoid all news

about the arts. There would be no danger of him turning a page and seeing a news article about the grand opening of Compania de Ballet de Casillas's new theatre that night. There would be no danger of him turning the page to be greeted with his estranged wife's striking face staring at him, *the* face of Compania de Ballet de Casillas.

The face of the ballet company owned by the two men he hated. The face he could not expel from his mind even though he refused to think about her. He'd had every last trace of her removed from the chateau and her studio door locked.

How dared she ask such a thing of him? She wanted him to put his vendetta aside when she didn't spare two thoughts for him outside their contracted hours?

I need you.

Of course she did. Just as his mother and his two closest friends had needed him, all of whom had only ever wanted him for what he represented or could give them and not for himself. He didn't add his father to that list. He had never pretended he needed him.

And then to say she'd wished she'd married Javier?

If that comment had been designed to cut through him it had...

Suddenly he found his legs no longer supported him and he sat back down with a thud.

Freya was used to doing everything on her own and being single-minded. She'd *had* to dedicate her life to get where she was, turning her body black and blue in the process.

She had lost control in his office.

He had only ever seen her lose control before in the bedroom.

The rest of the time she was fully in command of herself and her actions. She never did or said anything without thought.

She *had* wanted to hurt him with that comment.

Because he had hurt her, he realised with a rapidly thumping heart.

She had come to him for help. She had *begged* him.

Freya had never asked for anything from him before but his jealousy over her love and commitment to her job, his automatic disbelief that she should need him, added to his fury at what she had asked of him, had all done the talking for him. And the thinking.

She was going to star in the most important performance of her life that night and she was terrified.

His beautiful, fiercely independent wife was terrified.

But how could she need *him*?

And after everything he had done to her.

He had called her selfish but that was far from the truth.

He was the selfish one.

He'd been wrong to think she should change habits formed over a lifetime just to suit his ego in a marriage she had never wanted to a man she had never wanted.

And he was wrong to allow his vendetta to destroy her life.

Slumping forward, he rubbed at his temples and willed the drums and cymbals crashing in his head to abate.

He willed the throbbing ache in his heart to abate too. He had been willing that since he had watched her be driven out of his life.

The press would be out in force that night and the spotlight would be on her, the heir to Clara Casillas's throne.

She would see Javier that night too. Everyone would be watching them both to see how the mercurial Javier Casillas dealt with the dancer who had dumped him for his oldest friend.

No one knew their marriage was already over. Over…

He had thrown her out.

The banging in his head got louder, his chest tightening so hard he could no longer draw breath.

Dear God, what had he done?

Freya would have to deal with all the press attention and Javier on her own while trying to find a way to get her unwilling body to do the performance of its life.

How could he let her go through that alone?

She *did* need him.

She needed him to fix the damage he had caused with his bitter selfishness and untrammelled jealousy.

Freya sat at her dressing table applying colour to her whitened cheeks. She liked to do her own hair and make-up before a performance, liked that she had a private dressing room in which she could concentrate on nothing but her breathing. She was fully warmed up, her costume had been fitted and in two minutes she would join her fellow dancers in the wings. From the apprehension she found whenever she looked in anyone's eyes, they were as terrified about her performance as she was.

Strangely, admitting her feelings for Benjamin had had a positive effect on her psyche. It had been like removing the weights that had turned her limbs to lead. She felt sicker in her stomach but freer in her arms and legs. She could only pray it translated to the stage.

She blinked rapidly and dragged her thoughts away from Benjamin before the tears started up again.

No tears tonight, Freya, she told herself sternly.

A short knock on the door was followed by one of the stagehands poking her face into the room. 'More flowers for you.'

Her dressing room was already filled with enough bouquets to open her own florist's and this was the largest bunch by a clear margin.

Accepting them with a forced smile, she was about to put them on her dressing table when she caught the scent of lavender.

She put her nose into the bunch, closed her eyes and inhaled deeply, memories of Provence and Benjamin flooding her.

Lavender was the scent she would always associate with him. If she made it to old bones she already knew it was a scent that would still hurt her.

Her hands shook as she sniffed again and looked at the bunch properly.

Flowers of all different colours and varieties were in the beautiful bouquet but overwhelming it all were purple lavender flowers.

Placing the bouquet on her lap, she fought her fingers to open the envelope they had come with.

You are a shining star, ma douce. *Every heart will belong to you tonight but mine will beat the strongest.*

Her heart thumping, she stared around the small dressing room as if he would suddenly appear.

Did that mean he was here?

'Who gave you these?' she asked the stagehand, who was still at her door.

'A tall man in a tuxedo.'

'That narrows it down,' she said with a spurt of laughter that wasn't the least bit humorous. Every person there would be dressed in their finest clothes. 'Can you be more specific?'

The stagehand's face scrunched up in thought. 'Black hair. Thick eyebrows. Scary-looking.'

It *was* him!

Benjamin was here!

She could hardly believe it.

Joy and dread converged together to set off a new kaleidoscope of butterflies in her belly.

He was here! Here to support her. Under the same roof as the two men who had caused him such harm for *her*.

The stagehand looked at her watch. 'They're waiting for you.'

With a start, Freya realised she was in danger of missing her cue.

She ran to the wings, whispering her apologies to everyone she passed.

The orchestra played the opening beats and then it was time for the performance to begin.

From the private box Benjamin, who had paid an extortionate amount of money to procure it from a richly dressed couple in the theatre lobby, large glass of Scotch in hand, watched Freya dance on the stage with more pride than he had ever known he possessed.

Seeing her in her studio practising alone and clips on the Internet were no substitute for what he witnessed now, beauty expressed in its purest form, a witty portrayal of ambition and a heart-wrenching portrayal of love.

Freya flew as if she had wings. No one else watching would believe the pain she put her feet and limbs through to create something so magical and here, seeing it with his own eyes, he understood for the first time why she put herself through the torture.

She captivated him and, from the faces in the rows below him, she had captivated everyone else too. When the tragedy at the end occurred he doubted there was a dry eye around.

He sipped the last of his Scotch to burn away the lump that had formed in his throat.

If anything were to happen to Freya for real…

It would kill him.

She wouldn't give him a second chance, he knew that. He didn't deserve it and wouldn't ask for it. But as long as he knew she was living the life she had worked so hard for and creating the magic he had witnessed that night, he could live his own life with some form of peace.

It was only as he left the box to search for her and caught sight of Javier and Luis that he realised he hadn't thought about either of them once that evening. His entire focus had been on Freya.

This could be his moment, he thought, heart thumping, blood pumping. The opportunity to punch them both in their treacherous faces, to show his utter contempt for them with the world's press there to witness it in all its glory...

He turned on his heel and walked in the other direction.

Freya accepted the warm embraces from her colleagues and told them, one after the other, that no she wouldn't be attending the after-show party but yes, of course she would keep in touch.

The best embrace had come from Mikael, who had thrown her in the air before planting a massive kiss on her lips. 'I knew you could do it!' he had said in his thick Slavic accent. 'You were magnificent!'

And then she had set off to the privacy of her dressing room reflecting that this would be the last time she would walk these corridors. There was none of the sadness she'd expected that this chapter of her life was over.

She still didn't know what her future held dance-wise. She'd put everything on hold to get through that performance.

And she had done it!

She felt giddy. And sick.

Because the other part of her future was also an unknown.

Now the euphoria of the performance was dissipating, the relief at having Benjamin there somewhere within the packed theatre was leaving her too.

If there was any chance he had feelings for her, and her gut told her he did, she knew it wasn't enough for them. How could it be when they both wanted and needed such different things?

Their ending had been fated from their beginning. How could any union forged on hate ever end in anything but disaster?

But still she longed to see him.

Where was he?

Would he seek her out?

She had no idea how she would react or what she would say if he did.

Her heart sank to find her dressing room empty of everything but the dozens and dozens of bunches of flowers. They would be forwarded to her apartment in the morning.

By the time she'd stripped her costume and make-up off and donned a pair of skinny jeans and a black shirt her heart had fallen to her feet.

He hadn't sought her out.

Unnoticed by anyone, she slipped out of the theatre and hailed a taxi.

The short journey to her apartment took for ever.

Had she imagined the note from Benjamin? If she hadn't then where was he? Why had he not come to find her?

So lost in her desolate thoughts was she that when she stepped out of the elevator across from her apartment, she almost didn't register the figure sitting on the floor by her door.

The keys she had in her hand ready to let herself in almost slipped through her fingers

Benjamin lifted his head and stared at the woman he had been waiting for.

He got to his feet while she walked slowly towards him. Her face didn't give anything away but her eyes…they were filled with a thousand different emotions.

'I apologise for leaving the theatre without seeing you,' he said, breaking the silence. 'Javier and Luis were there. I didn't want to create a scene so thought it best to leave before anything could happen. Please, can I come in?'

She inhaled then nodded and unlocked the door with a shaking hand.

'Can I get you a drink?' she asked politely, no longer looking at him.

Grateful that her first words to him weren't of

the *get the hell out* variety, he answered with equal politeness. 'If it isn't too much trouble.'

'Wine?'

'You have alcohol?'

Her gaze darted to his. The glimmer of a smile quirked on her lips. 'I had a glass last night. There's three quarters of the bottle left.'

'You will have a glass with me?'

'Do I need it?'

'Probably. I know I do.'

A sound like a muted laugh came from her lips but the way she tore her eyes from him and blinked frantically negated it.

In the kitchen, she opened the tall fridge and pulled out a bottle of white. She took two glasses out of a cupboard, filled them both virtually to the rim and took a large drink from one. She gestured for him to take the other.

So she didn't want to risk touching him. He could not blame her for that.

'You were wonderful tonight,' he said softly. 'I could not take my eyes off you.'

A hesitant smile played on her lips. 'Thank you. It helped knowing you were there. I know it must have taken a lot.'

'Do not dare thank me,' he said darkly. He did not want her gratitude. He downed the rest of his wine and put the glass down on the counter.

Her eyes had become wary. 'Benjamin…?'

He held out a hand to stop her. 'First, let me apologise unreservedly for the way I spoke to you and for throwing you out of my home.'

'You hardly threw me out. You got your driver to take me to the airport.'

'Do not make excuses for me.' He glared at her. 'I do not deserve excuses and I will not accept them. My behaviour, everything I have done to you has been abhorrent. I will not make excuses to myself any more. I *did* steal you from Javier. I have been a jealous fool. I saw you in Javier's garden and have not been the same since.'

'What do you mean?' she asked in a far softer tone than he deserved.

'Something happened to me when I first set eyes on you. I could not get you from my mind. I was obsessed with you. I wanted you for myself because I am a selfish, greedy man. I chose you as leverage against Javier, not because I thought it was the most effective way to get my money back but to destroy your engagement.'

'You wanted to destroy us?'

He gave a tight nod. Since making the decision to go to Madrid to support her, he had done nothing but think. It had not been a pleasant awakening.

'I could not bear to think of you in his bed or him touching you,' he told her. 'I salved my conscience by telling myself you were better off without him, but you were right that time when you asked me who I thought I was deciding what was right for you. And you were right that everything I did was to serve my own agenda. *You* were my agenda. If you weren't I would have paid you off when you suggested it. I would have done anything to have you and make you mine. And now I would do anything to make amends. I don't deserve or expect your forgiveness. I have ruined your life. Javier would have been the better man for you to marry, and I do not say that lightly. He would never have tried to control you or influence where you worked.'

'Only because he wouldn't have cared,' she interjected with a whisper.

'But that is what you need, is it not? The freedom to live your life for what is best for you and your career without anything else fighting for space in a life already full with your dance and your parents? I took that away from you. I made what should have been the greatest night of your life a nightmare. When you reached out to me about your troubles I pushed you away because I didn't believe an independent woman like you, who has never needed anyone, could need me when no one has ever needed me before. I was jealous too, of you living under the same skies as Javier, and jealous you had a passion that didn't involve me.'

'You were jealous of me dancing?'

'*Oui.* Your dance. It is who you are, *ma douce.* It is one of the reasons I fell in love with you.' Her eyes widened at his casual admission but he carried on, wanting to get everything off his chest while he had the chance. 'When you commit to something you do not do it lightly. I cannot tell you how much I admire the dedication and commitment it must have taken you to become the woman you are today or how envious I am of the childhood you had.'

'You're jealous of my childhood? What on earth for? We were dirt poor.'

'But rich with love. My father left when he couldn't take playing second fiddle to Clara Casillas any longer—and to think I am anything like him just destroys me—and my mother...' He breathed heavily. This was an admittance he had barely acknowledged to himself. 'She loved me in the way an owner loves its pet. I was an accessory, conceived as a playmate for the children Clara would have. When Clara died she transferred her love to Clara's sons. I could never make her smile the way they did. When my father left he didn't give me a second thought and I didn't give him one either. That's what I mean about never being needed before.

'Your parents love you. Whatever career path you chose they would have done anything they could to support and encourage you whatever the cost to themselves. And you are the same. When you love someone you give them your whole heart and I will never forgive myself for making you a pawn in my vengeance.'

He paused to get some air into his lungs.

Freya was staring at him, eyes wide, her mouth half open but no sound coming out.

'You will have seen the deposit I made into your account. It's the sum I should have paid you to begin with rather than force you into a marriage you did not want. Anything you want, for you or for your parents, message me—I don't expect you to call. I know I can't make things better by throwing money at it but, for the sake of my conscience, promise you will always come to me. I need to be able to sleep again, *ma douce*, and abandoning my plans for revenge on Luis isn't enough.'

She smiled weakly. 'You're going to leave Luis alone?'

'I have done enough damage to spend eternity in hell. I will let his own conscience punish him.'

Her chin wobbled. 'I'm glad. And I'm proud of you.'

'I do not deserve that,' he said with a grimace.

'You could have made a scene tonight but you didn't. You walked away. Your soul isn't a lost cause, whatever you believe.'

'I only walked away because of you. You are more important to me than anything. More important than my hate for them. I can only apologise again and again that it was nearly too late for your performance before I realised it.'

'But it wasn't too late, was it? You were there. You came. That means the world.'

He managed the semblance of a smile. 'You have a beautiful heart, *ma douce*. I hope one day you find a man deserving of it.' He took one more deep breath and gave a sharp nod. 'And now I shall leave you to your rest.'

Stepping over to her, he put his hands lightly on her shoulders, breathing in the scent he had missed so badly for the last time. Brushing his lips to her forehead, he whispered. *'Au revoir, mon amour.'*

He took comfort that she didn't flinch away from his touch.

Holding his frame together by the skin of his teeth, he walked to the door.

He would fall apart when he was in the privacy of his home. There was a whole bar full of Scotch for him to drown his sorrows in.

'So that's it?' she called after him, stopping him in his tracks. 'You come here to pour your heart out and tell me you love me and then *leave*? What about all the things I need to say to you?'

He closed his eyes. 'Whatever you need to say, I will listen.'

'You can start by turning around and facing me.'

Slowly he turned, expecting to see anger, preparing for the full-scale verbal attack he deserved.

Instead...

Instead he was greeted by the softest, gentlest expression he had ever seen.

She treaded over to him and placed a hand on his cheek. 'I took one look at you in Javier's garden and I fell in love with you. I was obsessed with you. I couldn't stop thinking about you even though they were thoughts I knew I shouldn't have. When you stole me away...' She sighed. 'I have tried my hardest to hate you. There have been times when I *have* hated you but running beneath it all has been my heart beating harder than it has ever beaten before because it is beating for two. It is beating for you. I lost my ability to dance because my heart and soul became yours without my knowing. I could only dance in the chateau because that's where you were. I needed to be near you. I still need to be near you. I can dance again now, I found a way through it, but without you in my life the passion is lost. I do need you, Benjamin. Like a fish needs water. I can't breathe properly without you.'

Her lips found his to press the most tender of kisses to them.

She sighed again. 'I love you. When I dance it is your face I see before me and it lifts me higher than I have ever jumped before. You make me want a life that's more than dance. You bring all the different colours and flavours of life out in me.'

He didn't dare allow joy anywhere near him. 'But can you forgive me? Can you ever trust me?'

'I *do* trust you. As for forgiveness, I can promise to forgive you if you can promise to forgive yourself.'

'I don't know how,' he answered honestly. He would never lie to her.

'By drawing a line in the sand on the past. What's done is done and we can't change it. All we can do is look to the future and the only future I want is with you.'

'The only future I want is with *you*. Without you I am nothing. I will follow you anywhere. To the ends of the earth. You can dance in China for all I care, I will be there with you.'

She kissed him again. 'Then prove it to me.'

'How?'

'By loving me for ever.'

Suddenly feeling as if his heart would burst, Benjamin finally allowed himself to believe...

She loved him! This incredible woman who could move his heart with the tilt of her head loved him.

In his wildest fantasies he had never allowed himself to think that.

But she did. And he loved her.

Parting his lips, he kissed her back with all the love and passion she had filled his heart with, thanking all the deities in the skies for giving him this second chance to be a better man with this woman who completed him.

And he would love her for ever.

EPILOGUE

Terror clutched at Benjamin's heart.

That was his wife, waiting in the wings, ready to come on stage and dazzle the packed theatre of families at the Orchestre National de Paris in her role as the Sugar Plum Fairy for this one-off Christmas production of *The Nutcracker*.

And this was their year-old son asleep on his lap, blissfully unaware his mother was about to perform for the first time since his birth. And in such a monumental, iconic role too.

It would also be her first performance since her mother had died peacefully in her sleep that summer. Freya and her father had consoled themselves that they had been given another two years with her, good years with months in which she'd been well enough to travel to Russia and New York and watch her only daughter guest star with some of the most famous ballet companies in the world and meet her first grandchild.

Benjamin had no idea how Freya was going to pull it off. His darling wife had had a roller-coaster year with tears and laughter, sadness and joy. All the ups and downs had only brought them closer together.

Freya was his world. Christopher, the dark-haired bundle of mischief in his arms, had completed them.

Gasps from the children in the audience brought him back to the present, and he blinked to see the vision in a glittering white tutu take to the stage.

Then the familiar tinkling music began and his wife transformed into the Sugar Plum Fairy.

With subtlety, charm and grace, she moved over the stage, that illusion of flight she did so perfectly enthralling the whole spellbound theatre.

'She's wonderful,' whispered his father-in-law, sitting beside him in Benjamin's private box.

Benjamin nodded his agreement, too choked to speak. He didn't have to look to know Freya's loving father had tears rolling down his face.

When the orchestra played its final note in the dance, the theatre erupted. Cheers and bellows rang out, a sound so different from what had played before that Christopher woke up.

Bouncing in excitement, he pointed to the stage. 'Mama!'

'*Oui*, that's your mama,' Benjamin whispered into his son's ear. 'And your grandfather is right— she is wonderful.'

* * * * *

If you enjoyed the first part of Michelle Smart's
RINGS OF VENGEANCE *trilogy,*
BILLIONAIRE'S BRIDE FOR REVENGE,
look out for the following instalments,
coming soon!

And, in the meantime, why not explore her
BOUND TO A BILLIONAIRE *trilogy?*

PROTECTING HIS DEFIANT INNOCENT
CLAIMING HIS ONE-NIGHT BABY
BUYING HIS BRIDE OF CONVENIENCE

Available now!